BOOKS BY
RENATE STENDHAL

Sex and Other Sacred Games (*with Kim Chernin*)

Gertrude Stein in Words and Pictures

Cecilia Bartoli: The Passion of Song
(*with Kim Chernin*)

The Grasshopper's Secret

Love's Learning Place: *Truth as Aphrodisiac
in Women's Long-Term Relationships*

The
GRASSHOPPER'S

SECRET
A MAGICAL TALE

RENATE STENDHAL
with illustrations by the author

EDGE
WORK

The Grasshopper's Secret — A Magical Tale

Copyright © 2002 by Renate Stendhal

EdgeWork Books
Boulder, CO 80302
www.edgework.com
For orders, call 800-773-7782

Illustrations and cover art: Renate Stendhal

Cover and book design: Michael Brechner / Cypress House

Library of Congress Cataloging-in-Publication Data

Stendhal, Renate.
     The grasshopper's secret : a magical tale / Renate Stendhal ;
with illustrations by the author.
         p. cm.
     Summary: When thirteen-year-old Zelda travels through time
     and space to Venice, Italy, her actions help a young boy she
     had envied, thereby changing her relationship in the present
     with him, with her family, and with herself.
     ISBN 1-931223-05-X (casebound : alk. paper)
     [1. Time travel--Fiction. 2. Magic--Fiction. 3. Interpersonal
relations--Fiction. 4. Grasshoppers--Fiction. 5. Venice
(Italy)--Fiction. 6. Italy--Fiction.] I. Title.
     PZ7.S8287 Gr 2002
     [Fic]—dc21
                                                   2001053257

Printed in the United States of America by Thomson-Shore.

First Edition
2   4   6   8   9   7   5   3   1

For Zelda, of course

ACKNOWLEDGEMENT

Hats off to my first and youngest reader, Jessica Roach, who at age eleven was already a keen editor. Her comments gave a welcome spin to the Grasshopper's next hops.

CONTENTS

PART I

THE SECRET

CHAPTER 1

"Forty minutes, twenty-one seconds late." Zelda counted on her watch. Her mother came rushing in, her auburn curls in a tousle. She threw her jacket and briefcase on the sofa. Zelda and her father were doing the Saturday lunch dishes.

"We left some soup for you on the stove," her father called through the open kitchen door.

Her mother joined them, a stack of mail in her hands. "Hungry as a wolf," she said and kissed her husband on his lips.

"Yuk," Zelda waved her dishtowel at her.

"Don't you worry," her mother said. "You'll come to like it soon enough."

"YUK!" Zelda repeated.

"I don't get it." Her mother filled a bowl with soup. "When I was her age I couldn't grow up fast enough."

"Isn't it quite normal, Ellen, nowadays?" Zelda's father asked.

"I TOLD you," Zelda rose above them. "I am eight years old and I'll never be a day older."

"Of course." Her mother rolled her eyes. "A teenager who wants to stay a baby. When will you stop that nonsense?"

Zelda stared her down with a squint. She hated the word teenager. She hated the whole idea of breasts and boys. "Eight," she shouted with the perfect intonation of a child. "I am eight, eight and eight!"

Impatient, her mother took her bowl and headed to the stack of files on the living room table. "At least there's one normal kid in the family." She winked at the small blond boy who had come in from the garden. "Tell her she's thirteen and should be proud of it."

Zelda had not forgotten that only a few days ago he had said to her, "I also am eight, too," his eyes blue with admiration. Now he said, "I'm mostly eleven," and blushed.

"Almost," Zelda's mother corrected him from the living room.

Zelda studied him from the corner of her eyes. Her mother had brought him back from one of her trips abroad, a lost sheep in need of a fold. He was from somewhere in Europe, but Zelda didn't care to remember the details. Apparently his parents didn't want him. Or they never had time. That was familiar.

"It's up to you," her mother had said. "If you can't learn to be more sociable, we are sending you to your cousins' for a while." Zelda had been "getting out of hand," always fighting with her mother and swearing like a thug. She couldn't help it. Something about her mother just made her mad all the time.

But going to live with Dolly and Becky and Sue was the last thing she needed. Their brains had recently shrivelled to two topics: boys and clothes, clothes and boys. And they were tattletales who would report everything about her back to her mother. It would be easier to keep her secrets from a stranger who was half a baby anyway. But what had her parents imagined? That this lost sheep would stop her?

He should have come to stop her mother. Or at least distract her. That's what Zelda had hoped for. But he hadn't got Zelda off the hook. He'd made her look worse. He didn't swear or curse or put up fights. He didn't have ugly copper wire curls; he was blond and cute. And he had a pet name that everyone except her found adorable: Kidcou. It was French. Her father had explained that it was short for Kid Courage. It had to be pronounced *coo-raajh* because it was French although he wasn't French. Her mother had told her there was a reason he had that name. Why didn't Zelda ask him about it?

It wasn't fair. She had watched the lost sheep struggle to set foot in his new world. She had seen him make a fool of himself countless times, but her mother hadn't caught on. Whatever he messed up, there was always the excuse that he was a stranger who couldn't possibly know. And if for once there was no excuse, there were still his eyes.

He had a way of looking up from under his lashes when he was hurt or ashamed, and his eyes played a trick on you. They got bluer than blue, turning moist, like tears. It made it hard to go after him, and this must be why her mother never did.

When she was alone with him, Zelda liked to egg him on, "Try mean-eyes, Kits. Come on, try!"

He would squint, trying to imitate her power stare. His girl-like lashes would quiver and the blue would flash, reminding her of Blue Nile stones, fake gems her mother had offered her in third grade as a reward for staying home alone at night. The girls in her class, and even some of the boys, had been wild about Blue Nile stones. One day, in a rage, Zelda had washed all of hers down the drain. She should have bartered them for a white mouse or some other pet her mother hated.

Everything had changed. She wasn't alone any more all day, with her mother out on some legal campaign and her father shuttling back and forth between his college office and the steaming greenhouse in the back of the garden. It had been a new game to tease Kidcou or, in a generous mood, teach him. He hadn't known how to take the bus, spot a mailbox, make a call from a phone booth, or get himself an ice cream. Watching him order "a ball of strawberry fudge" had been a thrill at first. But he had caught on. He'd started imitating her every move, ordering everything she got for herself. Suddenly the fun had worn off. It was maddening to always have him waiting around for her, always wanting to know what she wanted so he could want it, too.

"Dad, when will we go back to living like we used to? Just the three of us?"

They were finishing the dishes. Kidcou was back in the garden, her mother was on the phone.

The greying tufts of her father's eyebrows went up. "What's wrong, dear?"

"Don't they want him there, in Europe? Won't he have to go back soon?"

"Are you saying you don't like Kidcou?"

She could tell she had disappointed him. "Dad, he's just a crybaby. It doesn't make sense. I don't need him, and I know I'm not doing him any good."

He leaned in as if to tell her a secret, "The destiny of our best friends is often in our own hands."

She made a quick move away. "He's not my friend!"

Her father studied her. "You know, dear, your mother and I are convinced that you've been lonely far too long."

Zelda knew it was useless. She wasn't lonely at all. She had her baseball team. She was going to practice more often than ever. Baseball was something Kidcou just couldn't do. True,

she didn't hang out much with the boys, but that was because she liked being alone. And because it didn't make sense
to bat the ball with a fury so the boys had to scramble after
it, only to have her hand held by one of them afterwards at
the ice cream parlor. Her father wouldn't understand. Or, if
he did, he would give her his sad look or come up with another one of his sayings about friends that never told her
what she needed to know.

She finished her lunch chores and left the house unseen.
She went roaming through the back alleys of the neighborhood. Rolling her tongue around a piece of candy, she knew
something was about to happen.

She had first known it on the day she had escaped from
the birthday party her mother had organized. Her eighth
birthday. She had always hated to wear a dress and stand
on a chair at the head of a long table while everyone bel-
lowed, "Happy Birthday, dear Zelda!"

That day, the day she turned eight, she had stayed in the
alleys until she was sure nobody was still around to watch
her open their silly gifts. She had promised herself never to
have another birthday. She had wished it so hard, harder than
anything she ever wanted. "Give me a sign," she had pleaded.
"Tell me I never have to grow up and become like my mother.
Give me this, please. Give me a sign."

She hadn't been sure who she was talking to, but something had happened. Right then and there, in the dirty back
lanes, she had found a treasure. A piece, then another, of
mysteriously beautiful glass. Someone must have heard her.
It was the sign: a gift that mattered because it appeared in
the dirt and gravel.

8

It happened again. And again. Year after year, they showed up. Not the ugly everyday stuff of broken beer bottles; old glass pebbles, seasoned by time and weather. Stepped on by blind feet. Ground into sand and gravel and pushed back to the surface over and over. Buffed and baked by the sun. Pale green, her favorite color. Clouded blue when it was her day of special omens.

Recently, it had become an almost daily hunt. Her parents didn't have a clue that she didn't do much of her homework, and sometimes even cut class. She made sure Kidcou didn't have a clue either. She kept her treasure in a cigar box in her school locker. Her teammates and other kids at school believed she picked them up at a special beach somewhere, but that would have been too easy. She never told them, and the kids at school were always after Zelda's smoky-smelling good-luck charms.

A few alleys later, she held a water-green piece of glass up against one eye. It was smooth and flat enough to look through. Everything around her was water-green. She kept walking, scanning from side to side. When she almost closed her eyes she could see a city, built in the ocean. She knew the city from her *Illustrated Legends of the Sea*, the book her father had given her the night before her eighth birthday. Houses, their feet in the water. A boat.

She pressed the piece of glass closer to her eye. She squinted. Now she was riding in a boat along a narrow canal, under one low stone bridge, then another. Water was lapping against the hull, sounding like spoons smacking into jello. The air was still. She knew she was after something. Something was hidden in the black boat she saw gliding ahead of her at a distance.

9

She almost jumped when she made out the silhouette. A figure was suddenly standing in the boat — the tall, slender figure of a woman. The Rower. The Rower was the Empress of the Sunken City. Zelda knew her from her book where she was also called Our Lady of the Canals. The Rower, it was said, drove her boat without touching the oars. She simply willed its course.

Zelda strained her eyes against the glass. The Rower seemed to be wearing a long water-green gown, but it could also be a cape or a raincoat. She followed the Rower around a corner into a maze of canals between musty old houses and crumbling garden walls. She took care not to look too closely and not to get too close. It could be dangerous. If you followed the Rower uninvited and she turned around and caught you, you were finished. But if she liked you, the book said, she would guide you to a treasure.

The Rower seemed to know exactly where she was headed. But where? One might have to follow her forever to find out. Zelda kept up with the boat from canal to canal, until the sun was low, until she reached the brick wall next to the dusty palm tree where the canal went underground and where, right at this moment, a black dog turned around the corner of the alley.

She picked up a sharp-edged stone and scratched a boat into the brick wall. She couldn't tell Kidcou. You had to watch out with him. Just telling him a little about anything could turn his eyes into blue pits. Tell him about the Rower? Or even about the canals? What if he laughed his head off the way he did, so that it was hard to resist him — his nose crinkled, his blond bangs thrown stiff into the air? What if he didn't laugh, but started pestering her about being taken along? Or tried to spy on her and then secretly followed the Rower on his own? Zelda stuck another piece of candy between her teeth, squinting. You had to squint hard to prevent your secrets from being sucked into Kidcou's eyes.

She knew he'd be waiting for her to come home. Sure enough, he was riding his bike up and down the street, practicing acrobatics.

"Zeldi!" He waved. "Look!" He was steering with his feet on the handlebar.

"Zeld*A*!" she pronounced.

"Where have you been all the day?" He jumped off and parked his bike in front of the house.

She drew her mouth into a grin. "Things to do all the day, what else?"

"What things? I have waited for you after lunch. I thought we could play or something."

"Yeah. Play dead." Zelda slid the glass pebble into her Bermudas' pocket and kept watch on the pits in his eyes. A quiver of doubt came up, and she wished she didn't have to be mean.

"If you tell me, I tell you, too," he proposed. "I found a hummingbird. It's dead — I saw it die!"

"Okay. You show me first. I never saw a dead one.''

Kidcou led her past the greenhouse to what he called his "garden," a patch of pansies and moss under paper sunshades.

"I was puttering in my garden. Suddenly, I heard a thump on the glass roof. I thought some idiot guy had thrown a stone! But nothing came rolling down. Nothing. So I went in — look!" He opened the glass door and pointed.

11

The bird lay peacefully on its side: the body green, the head with its long beak, and the tip of its wing shimmering turquoise and blue. The tiny claws seemed to grip the air.

"A hummingbird all right."

"Can you imagine a bird like that making a thump like a stone? I thought they weigh nothing at all. Just feathers."

"That's death," Zelda declared. "Death makes things heavy. It probably was already dead when it came down. Right out of flying. These birds never sit, never sleep. And when they die they just fall out of the sky." She wasn't sure this was true, but it sounded good.

"Let's get the ladder, let's do! I've been waiting for you all the day."

Zelda suddenly remembered how she resented Kidcou's fussing over those birds, mixing one sugar solution after another to attract them, and running out every few minutes to check.

"I wouldn't touch it," she said. "Might be poisoned."

"Poisoned?"

"Well, you know how people use all kinds of weird sweeteners in their feeders…"

Kidcou's gaze leapt over to one of his own feeders in the peach tree. "They are too smart, Zeldi. If it's not good what is in the feeder, they don't come." There was a shadow over his face. "I try and try, but they never want to come and feed from mine."

Hearing him admit his failure changed her mood. She held the ladder while he climbed up. "Let's bury it under the quince. They like quince."

"We need a coffin." Kidcou studied the bird he held on a crinkled Kleenex. "Or perhaps the cats dig it out."

Zelda sped into the kitchen and emptied the big box of matches onto the table. Half of them spilled over her mother's dinner instructions. Kidcou had prepared a hole at the foot of the quince. He placed the bird on a bed of moss in the box.

"Why is it called hummingbird?" He fit the closed box into the hole and dribbled earth over it. "Birds sing, don't they? They don't hum?"

"Do you always have to ask questions? It's a name, that's all."

"But a name..."

"A name is a name. You don't have to do what your name says. You don't run around cooing, do you?"

"But it's French..." He looked hurt. "You just don't know about names."

"I was born in this country," Zelda said with dignity. "I know what's going on here. And remember, I've been eight years old for quite a bit longer."

"Eight plus eight plus eighty!"

She pushed her fist dangerously close to his face.

Kidcou ducked. He patted the earth of the little mound he had made. "It's not fair to fight at a grave. Let's do a good-bye song." When there was no protest, he began:

Hum hum hummingbird
now your humming is not heard,
I sing a song so you can be
forever here with me.

Zelda was unable to carry a tune, but she couldn't resist singing along with someone who could. She sang grudgingly:

Hum hum hummingbird
now your name is quite absurd.
I hum a hymn for you to be
forever loud in memory.

In spite of herself, she pulled the glass pebble out of her pocket. "For memory," she said, "we give you this. It's green like your feathers and the sun is inside it. Look!" She held it up for him. "Like sun on water, wouldn't you say?"

Kidcou's eyes marvelled.

"Like water in a canal." She put it to her eye like a monocle, peeping at him. "You don't walk along a street. The canal is the street. You can only go in a boat, even just to the next house."

Kidcou in turn looked through the piece of glass. "The houses grow out of the water. I know."

"You know?"

"I have seen it."

"What do you mean, you've seen it?"

"I've even seen the boat that comes to take the dead because they have no earth to bury them. Only water." He stuck the pebble on top of the little mound like a flag or gravestone.

"You, you can't have. How could you see that boat?"

"I went to live there awhile. But my uncle, he died."

"Live there. I see. One of your stories that no one can check on!"

"It's true! It was in Italy. Your mother was there. When she came to fetch me. In Venice."

"Sure. Somewhere on the moon."

"You only say that because you have never been there!"

"Me? Never been there?" Zelda snatched the glass pebble and balled her fist around it. "You don't know what you're talking about, buddy. You haven't really lived there, no way!"

"Well, not very long..." He seemed troubled. "But I saw the boat come for my Uncle Carlo, honest. After he died. It came right to our door. In my uncle's house, you could not use the down floor because it was always wet. You had to go down the stairs, and there was a pair of rubber boots for everyone. You had to put them on and wade to the boat. My uncle's boat was right next to the door, on the canal."

Zelda listened with suspicion. "What kind of a boat?"

"I don't know. Some motorboat. It was scary. It smelled strange in the house. Like mushrooms, like in a cellar. And what if the water would rise and rise all the way to our floor...? My Uncle Carlo said it wouldn't do that. Not in my lifetime. Scientifically unlikely, he said. But he showed me the brown lines on the wallpaper. That high the water had already been. Higher than my head!"

"Did you ever go in a boat ... by yourself, and follow a black boat with nobody inside?"

"Why would I do that?"

Zelda pressed the pebble to her lips before she placed it back on the mound. "Wherever you were is not where I was."

"But where, Zeldi? Where? Couldn't I have been there, too?"

No doubt about it. His eyes were blueing.

"There were black boats," he said after a moment. "Many black boats. Gondolas, they called them. But there was always someone in them. Even when they were empty."

"Even then?" She frowned. "Who?"

"A rower. Always. Many boats like that, everywhere."

"And the Rower," Zelda squinted, "looked how?"

"I don't know... He often had a black hat."

"*He*? The Rower a he?" Zelda slapped her thigh. "And many of those, lots and lots of them, you say?"

Kidcou looked confused.

"You must have had a bad dream." She gave him a playful punch. "Seeing things ... On the moon, yeah!"

"Leave me alone. I will never again tell you something."

He walked away with stiff legs, his fists in his pockets. She watched him plop down on his stomach by the terrace where a juniper hedge sheltered a small cage with a grasshopper. It was one of the few possessions he had brought with him. A brown suitcase with metal patches on the corners, and this cage. She had no idea why anyone would want a grasshopper for a pet. But right now she almost wished she had one.

Her father came down the path to the greenhouse with a tray of seedlings, wearing his blue garden apron.

"Everything all right?" he asked. Zelda could tell from his tone of voice that he had already guessed something was wrong.

"You bet, Dad." She watched her father bend over his rows of seedlings. Kidcou was propped on his elbows, his face next to the cage. After what seemed a decent amount of time, she strolled over to the hedge and sat down.

"Don't be mean, Kits. Normally you like it when people find your stories funny. I found your story funny. Just loved it."

He didn't look at her. He was holding a curved stalk of grass into the cage. To her amazement, she saw the grasshopper climb up the green bridge.

"This a circus act or something? Does it also bark?"

Kidcou looked immensely proud for a moment.

"Come on," she pushed. "Don't be a simp. I gave you my glass pebble for your hummingbird."

"What do you want?"

"Nothing. I like stories. Why don't you tell me some more? About the wet house and all. What other funny things did you see?"

He gave her a smoldering look. "I wish I could have stayed there ... "

Zelda nodded. She quite agreed.

"With my uncle Carlo. He had the funniest spectacles. The legs always came off, but he fixed them with bits of string." He raised two fingers next to his eyes.

"Like snail horns," she grinned.

"He had a big laboratory with a microscope and strange creatures in glasses. Specimens they were called. Some were snakes! He studied plants and nature and all. He taught me. He never sent me away. He said I could have his grasshopper when he was — when he would take the boat one more time, he said, and never ... "

"Never return,"she nodded. "And he didn't. His last ride. He knew."

Kidcou hid his face in his arm. Zelda tried not to notice. He was still holding the stalk even though the grasshopper had climbed down again. She inspected the insect for the first time.

"Why keep a cricket in a cage? There are so many everywhere. And they don't sing or even hum. Don't you find that weird?"

"This one is special," he said, keeping his face hidden. "It's not a cricket. My uncle Carlo said, when I am very unhappy some day, somewhere, his grasshopper will help me. But I don't know how. I don't remember, and later I could not ask him anymore.'' His voice died.

"Don't be stupid now," Zelda said, imagining she was a kind uncle. "What he meant, of course, was that it would help to have a friend! They always say that."

Kidcou let go of the stalk and wiped his nose. "What did you mean when you said 'hummahim' in your song?"

"*Hum a hymn*, dummy. A hymn is bigger than a song. The kind they sing when someone's died. In any case, I like your uncle Carlos. He knew what he was talking about."

"Zelda!" There was her mother's voice from the kitchen, threatening thunder. "Zelda! Come here immediately!"

"Holy shoot! I forgot to turn on the oven." She punched her head. "That's your fault, with your stupid hummingbird!"

An hour later, Zelda's throat hurt from yelling. She had argued with her mother until the potatoes were ready. When another fight broke out during dinner, she ran to her room and banged the door shut. Now she and her mother were shouting through the locked door.

"Leave me alone!" Zelda shrieked. "You always make me the black sheep. Nobody else. Always me. Just shove it!"

"Watch your mouth!" her mother yelled back. "When will you learn to grow up and behave like a normal person?"

"When will you give me a chance?"

"If you expect to be babied for the rest of your life, you are in for a surprise."

"What surprise?"

"You'll see. You'll get no allowance until you've proven to me that you can act like a responsible person."

"Oh yeah. A responsible person. Without money!"

"I told you what I expect of you. If you act like a child, you'll be treated like one. That's only logical."

"So what's the surprise if it's only logical?"

"Don't take me for stupid, Miss Know-it-all. You won't go to camp, if that's what you need to be surprised. Kidcou will go by himself and you will stay here. We'll see if that —"

"You call yourself a lawyer?" Zelda screamed. "I pity your clients. I've never seen anyone so unfair. I hate you! I hate you!"

She didn't hear her mother's reply. Her head spun so fast she turned to the window and jumped. She ran through the garden and down the back alley, her feet pounding, *Won't go to camp, won't go to camp!* No way. Her mother had promised. Everyone was going to diving camp. All she'd done was forget to make dinner.

She ran around the block until her sides hurt. When she didn't feel rage any more she climbed back through her window and lay down on her bed. She grabbed her old *Illustrated Legends of the Sea* from the shelf and checked the chapter on the Rower. Venice, Italy. It troubled her that Kidcou had been in that very place and knew things about it that she didn't know. Kidcou had seen something. But he hadn't seen the Rower. The Rower had shown herself only to Zelda. It was Zelda who found the special glass in the alleys.

CHAPTER 2

The next day bad air hung in the house. Zelda was condemned to do the dishes until her mother had decided about her punishment. She stayed in her room until her parents, neighbors and some friends were gathered around the radio for the evening news.

"What's a ninny?" Kidcou asked her when she came through the living room.

"Gimme a piece of your cookie and I'll tell you."

"Zelda!" Her mother had an uncanny ability to listen to conversations while listening to the news.

"A ninny's a moonsheep. A moron. Let's go outside."

They sat down on the garden wall behind the greenhouse.

Kidcou studied his thumbnails. "I told her, you know. After you went out the window and she — "

"How'd you know?"

"I've seen you jump out before. But I did not tell her that. I said that it was my fault, mostly. I made you forget, with the hummingbird and all. That you helped me bury it. I said, couldn't she please let you off? I would do the dinner for a while, and I would still do the dishes, too."

Zelda shook her head very fast to throw out of her ears what had just got in. "You must be kidding."

"That's what your Mom said. She said to your father, 'Is he

another ninny or what?' She told me to leave this to her and not to worry about you …"

"She's a lawyer and she's so unfair." Zelda's fist bounced on the garden wall. "I don't get it. I just don't get it."

"My godfather was a lawyer, too. Before going into the Foreign Office."

"She heard you!" Zelda nudged him. "My mother heard you ask about the ninny!"

Kidcou fumbled some pieces of a chocolate chip cookie from his pocket and offered her the least melted bits.

"She's pretty mad at me now." She munched with determination. "If only I'd kept my mouth shut. It's so unfair. She promised to let me go to camp if I had straight As. And now — "

"But that's still so many weeks away. Until then she has forgotten, no?"

"You have to say, *by* then. You don't know her. She never forgets anything." She slung her arms around her knees and rested her chin on her knee. "I once put a butterfly into the drawer where she keeps her nightgown, and when she opened it, it came at her. She is dead-scared of moths. She never forgave me. Still talks about it."

"In a drawer?"

"So what?"

"That's mean! I love flutterbies. To put them in a drawer hurts them."

"Perhaps a cage also hurts a grasshopper. When it jumps."

"I know." He chewed on his thumbnail. "I worry about him."

"Why do you always say he? Does *he* wear pants or something?"

"It's a he. In my language, it is. He was my Uncle Carlo's

friend, and my uncle said he would help me one day. I wish I knew how to let him out and still keep him safe."

"Gotta get a leash, like for a dog. Parcel string, maybe."

"Once he escaped from my uncle. From his lab. My uncle almost had a heart attack. But I saved him."

"Your uncle?"

"I saved the grasshopper."

"Yeah, nothing safer than prison."

"But everything is bigger here, and he is smaller." Kidcou looked troubled. "He wouldn't know how to defend himself. Perhaps he doesn't understand the other grasshoppers' chirrup."

"Because they *chirrup* in English." Zelda was pleased with herself.

Kidcou ignored her. "He has me at least. I protect him. He is special. My Uncle Carlo said so."

"I wish I had an Uncle Carlo. But a grasshopper should live among grasshoppers. Maybe he already chirps English better than you and you don't even know."

"I wish I knew. If only my Uncle Carlo had told me the secret — "

Zelda shifted her chin to her other knee. "That grasshopper should have come with instructions. 'Supposed to help you.' Help you with what? Doing the dishes?"

Kidcou fidgeted.

"If only I could go away somewhere," Zelda said. "Far away. You're damn lucky your parents let you go to Italy..."

"I have no parents. My foster parents took me in when I was tiny. After my parents died."

"No parents? They aren't your parents?" Zelda sat very still. "But they'll take you back to live with them?"

"My foster father is always traveling. Always another country. He said it would be bad for me. For school. Too many languages and all. German and French and English are enough, he said. But I almost learned Italian ..."

"Yeah, and you almost learned Enklishhh." She caught herself. "You really don't have parents? Why didn't you tell me?"

"I thought you knew. You never asked."

"But who took care of you?"

"Everyone. My nanny. My aunts and uncles. I liked my Uncle Carlo ..."

Zelda saw aunts and uncles standing in line, waiting to get Kidcou back from Los Angeles.

"You don't know how lucky you are." She inspected Kidcou as though she had never seen him before. "I wish we could change places." She had a sudden urge to stop him from fidgeting. "I wouldn't hang around here. I'd go back in a minute." She had stopped him. "Come on, how about it? You could take my place here in this shoothole and have my mom all to yourself."

"I wish I had your mom," he burst out. "You hate her, but I want her even if she never has time and yells and is unfair!"

"You can have her right now! She prefers you, anyway. With your ninny ways. Can't wait to do the dishes and the cooking and the cleaning and the whatnot. Goody two-shoes. Love me, Mom! Love me, Mom!" She jumped off the garden wall and whirled around to face him. She couldn't tell whether he was going to cry or punch.

"And by the way, Buddy. My mom isn't always unfair. She's not like your foster father. The Foreign Office! My mom would never work for the people in power. She'd never twist the law for them. When someone burned a cross into our new neighbors' lawn because they were Black, my mom wouldn't have it. She called for a protest right away, and lots of people came. Even newspaper people. And I brought food to the neighbors' house, every day. We had a barbecue right out front, on their lawn. That's how fair my mom is. So you'd better not say anything about her, because — "

Something was knotting up her voice. She quickly turned and stomped back to her room.

CHAPTER 3

It was late. The house was quiet. Zelda noticed her father's snoring from across the corridor. She opened the shutters, taking care not to make any noise. The air was thick with heat. She climbed onto her desk and leaned against the window frame.

If only she could get away. Her mother kept her a prisoner and wouldn't let her go to camp. Her father wouldn't defend her. Kidcou's pleading for her with her mother had only earned him points for himself. All he needed to do was use his big, blue eyes.

She pulled a mirror from her desk drawer and threw her eyes open as wide as they would go. She braced the mirror between her knees and pulled her lids apart with both hands. An anxious monkey stared back at her. Who would want to look at that? Who would want to throw secrets into narrow, flat, brown eyes?

Mean-eyes, that's all she could come up with and her mother hated her for it. "Stop looking at me like that. You won't get your way, Miss Stubborn." But it was her mother who was stubborn and always had to win an argument. Even when Zelda refused to argue. "Don't give yourself airs, Zelda. You can't bewitch me with that look."

She flung the mirror into the garden. Her eyes stung. *Stop pitying yourself,* she heard a familiar voice in her head. She aimed a kick at the window frame. Her leg looked funny. Small. The leg of a child. Eight years old, not a day older.

There was another voice: *I am with you. You are not alone.*

"Hey there, Rower," Zelda whispered. "I need to talk to you. Tell me what to do. Tell me how I can keep my mouth shut and not yell and not be so mean. Especially to Kidcou."

There was no answer.

She listened hard, then she took her *Illustrated Legends of the Sea* and carefully unfolded the layers of newspaper and tin foil that kept the pages together. She pulled out a thin stack of notes from their hiding place. They all bore her handwriting, some in pencil, others in ballpoint. Some had a date. Some were addressed: *God, they say you don't exist — but just in case*, or, *To whom it may concern out there somewhere.* Most of them said: *Rower, Empress of the Sunken City, help me not get so mad and never let me grow up. Never. Zelda.*

Perhaps she had to try harder. She tucked a notepad and pen into her pajama pocket. Listening backwards into the house, she made sure there was still her father's faint snore. She swung her body over her desk and the window sill, and leapt down.

Nothing stirred. There was her mirror stuck in a bush of thyme. She gave it a kick in passing.

Under the cherry tree, she sat down and wrote: *Rower of the Thousand Canals, you are my one and only ally. I can't stand it much longer. I keep getting so mad and mean. Please guide me. PLEASE. Zelda.*

After a moment, she added, *P.S. I'll give you something. I promise.*

She pressed the folded paper to her chest for a moment.

Then she placed it on the ground and secured it with a pebble. Tapping the ground with her feet, her arms curling up and down like waves, she circled the tree. She croaked out a song:

Rower of Rowers,
don't look at me,
come and listen to my plea.
Take my madness far away
and let it stay there, let it stay.

After a while, she forgot the song and just hummed along with her steps. It was a good feeling to dig her heels into the dust. In spots, the earth was still warm from the sun, in others it was cool like water. She felt a presence. She did not turn, she did not look up. The Rower always came when she was called.

She tucked her note into her belt and climbed into the cherry tree. She tore a small hole in the paper and stuck the note between the leaves of her branch. The Rower would have the whole night to read it. She bent forward, hugging the branch. Her cheek touched the silk of the bark. Suddenly she felt tired.

What could she give to the Rower? What did she have to offer? She would have to think about it … tomorrow.

CHAPTER 4

Her note was gone. Zelda dropped her books under the cherry tree. She climbed up to make sure. Gone. She had been so tired after her night in the garden, she had forgotten all about the note. Someone had taken it, and that someone was probably not the Rower. She cursed.

What if her father had found it during his morning rounds through the garden, checking for parched plants? It would be just like him to check high up on a tree.

Her father or Kidcou. Kidcou had sneaked up on her before. He had watched her climb out of her window, her mother yelling on the other side of the door. He must have seen her in the garden last night and come down first thing in the morning while she was still asleep.

She gathered up her books and hid behind the greenhouse. Thieves always return to the scene of their crime. He would come home from school and go right back to the cherry tree, if only to see if by any chance there was another note. She'd catch him in the act.

Crouching behind the greenhouse, she began to feel like an egg in a pan, sunny-side up. Heat seemed to seep through the panes from the inside out. The house and garden were deserted. Neighbor dogs barked.

It was odd. For once, Kidcou wasn't home right after school.

She stared at the rows of seedlings her father had been experimenting with inside the greenhouse. How could anyone be interested in plants that took forever to grow, needing to be grilled in a hothouse? Perhaps it had been her father after all.

She entered through the glass door and looked around his planting table, bracing herself against the heat. Had he stuck it in his garden apron? Spying was hard work if you didn't discover a thing.

She returned to the cherry tree and searched the beds and bushes around it in case the wind had played a trick on her. Finally, she took off to the old railroad tracks.

She sat down on a tie, her arms wrapped around her knees, her head bent. Her father was sure to show her note to her mother. Couldn't they just leave her alone? Her mother would be happier without her. She wouldn't have to pick and yell at her, and have that pained, tired look that made Zelda want to yell even louder.

Now there would be another fight over her note. She could hear it already, the fuss over her "childish scribble."

Why hadn't the Rower protected her note? Her only ally. Her guide.

She wished the trains were still running on the old track with its mustard greens. She would make herself small so the driver wouldn't notice her. She scooped up a handful of dirt and sprinkled it over her head. Invisible. A tiny speck among all the specks of heat and dust.

There was a drop on her calf. She watched her tear fall, and roll, and disappear in the dirt. The Rower must be out there somewhere. She squinted at the distance. But where? Did she still have an ally?

It struck her so hard, she leapt to her feet. How could she have been such a dope? She had not fulfilled her promise! The Rower was waiting. She hadn't lost everything. Not yet. She just had to find the right gift for the Rower. She gave the mustard greens a good pat before heading home. She still had a chance.

"Where've you been? How on earth did you get so dirty?"

Her mother was on the phone, wearing a flowered dress and lipstick. She dropped the receiver, gesturing at Zelda and calling her husband to be her witness.

"Doesn't she know we're going out?" She picked up the receiver. "Excuse me, Maud. This girl ... You should just see her! Hold on — " She again addressed her husband, "We should really leave her at home. We're late already."

Zelda's father looked at his watch. "I think we can still make it, Ellen. Can you wash your hair and be presentable in five minutes, Zelda? I am sure Kidcou wouldn't want to celebrate without you, would he?"

Zelda saw Kidcou sitting on the sofa edge, ready to go. His bangs were slicked back with water. He looked like a bathed baby in his dress shirt. Zelda grimaced at his indifferent gaze. Cheat. Spy. It was the anniversary of his arrival in the States. Was she supposed to keep his calendar?

"I'm at my wit's end ..." her mother shouted into the telephone while Zelda raced up the stairs.

Twenty minutes later, they sat down at the table. Zelda's wet curls were dripping down her neck into a T-shirt that almost matched her fresh pair of Bermudas. She felt a good mood coming on. Kidcou had picked an Italian restaurant for his celebration. She had to give him credit for that.

"*O sole mio...*" Zelda's father hummed along with the jukebox while he studied the menu.

"Ed, please!" her mother said. "You're not exactly Caruso."

"Alas, alas ...Italians have the sense of music. Always singing, always *la musica*. Isn't that true, Kidcou?" He winked at him while his wife rolled her eyes and filled her glass with wine.

"Spaghetti or pizza, Dad? Spaghetti or pizza?" Zelda tugged at her father's sleeve.

"Spaghetti for me," she heard Kidcou declare before she herself had decided. "Spaghetti Napoli with Parmigiano."

He hadn't even looked at the menu. He was looking straight ahead, his chin raised. Outdoing her on purpose.

"Listen to that pronunciation," her father said. "I'll have the same even though I can't say it quite that well."

Zelda stared at Kidcou. How come he hadn't waited to want what she wanted? Was he telling her something, with his nose up in the air?

"I bet you could say it, too," she nudged her father, "if you wore wet spaghetti on your head."

Everybody laughed. Even Kidcou, who touched his slick hair and got red ears.

"She'll go far in life, you'll see," her mother shook her head, her eyes fond and a little red from the wine. Zelda fidgeted while her mother watched her. "If she ever decides to grow up."

Zelda ordered pizza, but felt some regret when Kidcou's spaghetti plate arrived. She couldn't stop watching him dig his fork in and pull out strands of gluey, red-sauced, Parmesan-specked spaghetti. With swift turns of his fork he wound strand after strand into tight balls that promptly and neatly disappeared into his mouth.

"I suppose you have to live in Italy," her father smiled, "in order to master spaghetti with such elegance."

He poured a sip of wine for Kidcou and Zelda to celebrate Kidcou's first year in America. They all clinked glasses. Kidcou demonstrated how a German uncle of his used to toast. He stood up straight as a broom, swung his glass to his chest, cocked his head as though to inspect the contents with his nostrils, then shot his arm forward while snapping to attention. "To the ladies!" he shouted. He pretended to empty the glass in one gulp, and sat down.

Zelda's parents and their table neighbors clapped and had him repeat the toast. Zelda loudly slurped the rest of her wine to make sure she wouldn't be counted among the ladies.

"I wonder, Kidcou, if you ever miss Europe?" her father asked.

"I miss it." Kidcou said, to Zelda's surprise. She had never heard him complain about anything. "I miss going to the glass island. With my cousin Vito."

"What glass island?" Zelda asked.

"Where they make the glass."

"I think Kidcou is referring to Murano," her mother said. "The island next to Venice, where all the famous Italian glass comes from. Kidcou has an eye for fine glass." She gave Kidcou the kind of deep look she sometimes gave Zelda's father.

Kidcou suddenly looked troubled. Her mother put a reassuring hand on his arm.

"What do you mean, 'fine eye for glass'?" Zelda was growing alarmed.

Kidcou took a breath. "When I was real small, in Vienna,

one day a glass blower came to my class. He blew into his stick and out came a swan, and then an elephant, and a ship, and a horse with a horn on his forehead. He made one for each of us. I got a swan. It was light blue, and I could look all through it. Like it was only made of air. I ran home with it. But I fell down and it broke."

"Oh no! What a shame," Zelda's parents said in the same moment.

"My swan was all gone to pieces. Because it was so thin nothing was left to show."

"But the glass island? The glass island?" Zelda kicked the legs of her chair.

"When Vito took me to the island he showed me the many, many swans they were making. All the glass blowers, I watched them. How they made something for the tourists and then gave it to them, like the man at school. I thought I was also perhaps a tourist, but Vito said, no, he would show me something much better. A treasure, and I wouldn't have to buy anything to get it. Then he took me behind the factories, and there was nobody, just dirt. That was where the glass blowers threw all the glass they couldn't use. Gold and pink and green and purple pieces and clumps and all. You could look through them like my swan, but also way, way into them because they were so thick and they were real crystal and they could never break."

"Ah, *Venezia!*" Zelda's father's eyes twinkled. "A place of miracles."

Zelda had a sinking feeling. Crystal? In colors she had never found in her alleys and might never find? "Did you take a lot?" she asked.

"I took so many I ripped my pockets!"

"Why didn't you show me? Where are they?"

Her mother looked at him expectantly, but he seemed to avoid her.

"Where do you keep them?" Zelda pushed. "Don't say you lost them, too!"

He studied his thumbnails. "I could not bring them. I didn't lose them. I — I don't have them any more."

"Oh noooo!" Zelda shrieked. "How could you be so stupid?"

"Now, now," said her father. "Let's not jump to conclusions."

"Perhaps Kidcou would like to tell us what happened?" Zelda's mother sounded concerned.

"I promised not to tell. When my Uncle Carlo got so sick … And then I … I had to leave."

"Kidcou, shoot! You can't just stop and not tell the end of the story. It's not fair!" Zelda protested.

He looked unhappy. "I promised."

"But a story's not a story without an ending! Why tell it to begin with if — "

"We can use our imaginations," Zelda's mother stopped her. "A promise has to be honored. My respect to you, Kidcou."

"But why? Why?" Zelda wanted to punch them all. How could they so easily accept what was unacceptable?

"Kidcou will find another treasure, I am quite sure," her father said.

"When I go back to Italy," Kidcou said fiercely, "I take a huge bag to the island!"

"Back to Italy. Indeed." Zelda's mother exchanged a glance with her husband. "But you like it here, don't you?"

Kidcou didn't answer. Zelda glared at him. To imagine an

island where you could bend down and pick up the finest glass — crystal glass — and take as much as you could carry. And that's where he had been. Why he? Why did he get everything? What was it about Kidcou that made her mother look at him the way she did?

"Is there anything here that would make you like it even better?" her father asked.

"I wish Z..." Kidcou hesitated. Zelda knew what he was going to say. She saw the look he shot her. "I wish there were more birds. There are no swallows."

"There aren't? Is that true, Ed? I never noticed."

"Just swallow if you need a — " Zelda caught her mother's raised eyebrows and stuffed her mouth with pizza crunch.

"There are also no nightingales here," Kidcou continued. "And the blackbirds don't sing, they shriek!"

"So what?" Zelda had almost finished chewing. "Why didn't you bring a bird in a cage? Why drag around this grasshopper that'll die from boredom in its prison?"

Kidcou looked at her in shock. So did her father. Her mother's forehead was dangerously clouded.

"I didn't mean it like that," she said quickly. "Sorry, okay? I'm sorry."

He slowly nodded.

"Perhaps you can help Kidcou find a bird, Zelda," her mother said in a tone of voice that left no room for discussion. "Everyone can slip. What matters is to catch and correct oneself. Remember that and I'll be proud of you."

Zelda would rather die than blush. She downed her glass of water. She watched Kidcou from the corner of her eyes. She had said sorry just in time and he had accepted her apology.

39

He seemed to accept anything. She suddenly knew why. He had lost his treasure. Now anything had to be better than nothing.

CHAPTER 5

Zelda went into Kidcou's room, determined to make a deal with him.

"You are the only one who could have taken my note. Come on, Kits." She held out a paper bag with a sugar cane for him.

"I don't have it." He showed her his empty palms.

"I know you have it. What's it to you? Don't you want some candy?"

"You can look if you like."

Something had changed. He was watching her from under his lashes as if he was having fun. After trying another time, she cursed and went for the door.

"Why is it so important, this piece of paper?" There were the pits again in his eyes.

"Never mind. You are too stupid to understand that."

"That's what you always say. Because you are sooo clever! So clever that you lose such an important thing!"

"I didn't lose it, stupid! Someone took it! Can't you get that into your sheep's brain?"

"If you don't have it anymore, you lost it, stupid!" He grimaced back.

"Ha! That's a joke or something? Very funny. Try again. I only lost a piece of paper. But look at you!" She felt a pleasant hissing inside her. "First your f— swan and then that whole damn treasure. All of it! And you come here with nothing. Nothing! You are so stupid it hurts!"

"See how mean you are?" Kidcou's eyes flashed with pain and scorn. "Even if I could I would not help you find your note! You are always mean. I knew it. You say sorry only to get something. Or to please your Mom so she lets you go to camp. Ask your Mom to help you find your piece of paper where you always say she found you: in the garbage!"

Zelda gasped, exalted. "I knew it, too. I knew how disgusting you are. I could offer you anything and you still wouldn't give me my note. You are even worse than mean. You are cruel! But you always pretend to be so good, don't you? Good little Kidcou, coo-coo! You are a liar. And a thief. You come here with nothing and you steal everything. And you think you'll get away with it? Not with me!"

She tore the sugar cane out of the paper bag, hurled it onto Kidcou's shag carpet, and stomped out.

She almost bumped into her mother, who had appeared in the door frame, speechless. Zelda ducked, escaping her mother's grip. Across the hallway in the living room, she saw her father's puzzled face rise above the newspaper. She sped into her room and, in a single leap, was out the window.

"You have to stand up to that girl!"

Zelda heard her mother's voice from Kidcou's room. She cursed under her breath. Her ankle was twisted. She squeezed it to numb the pain, crouching between the bushes. She wouldn't get far. She overheard Kidcou confessing that he was afraid of her. Her mother insisted he had to fight back.

Then there was her father's voice, concerned, eager to know what was going on. "You aren't unhappy here, are you?"

43

"She thinks where I come from is all stupid. She never — "

The bed squeaked as if someone had sat down.

"Doesn't want to know? About Europe?"

"She — doesn't like me."

"Oh nonsense, Kidcou!" Her mother was getting impatient. "Everyone likes you. But I know my daughter, and you have to understand her. Zelda is just like me. The more we love, the more we bark. How come you don't look right through her?"

"Is it true that Zelda is not your real daughter?"

"Now what new nonsense has that girl dished up?"

Zelda pressed her fists to her ears. She had to get away before she lost it. She bit her lips to shut out the pain in her ankle. She made it over to the cherry tree and climbed up. She waited. She listened to the hum of the late evening news, the rise and fall of her parents' voices debating. She heard them knock at her door to say good-night.

"Don't leave the garden, you know the rule," her mother shouted through the locked door. "We'll talk tomorrow."

"Sleep well," her father added.

The light in the bathroom window came on; Kidcou's reading lamp turned off. Then, finally, dark and silence.

The moon inched up, shoving its belly like a white whale. Zelda noticed a cricket stirring. Soon the "gzz-gzz-gzzz" rose around the garden and leapt across the fence. She slid down, hobbled over and reached through her window to fetch paper and pen from her desk. She had to take care of business. A moment later, a message wrapped around a pebble went flying through Kidcou's window into his room. It read: *I heard you with my parents. I'll never forgive you. Zelda.*

She rolled onto her stomach under the tree, her face in her

hands, trying to concentrate. A nuisance, these crickets. Especially the grasshopper. A pesterbody like his owner. Screeching day and night on a cello with only one string. Better not think of it. She had to fulfill her promise.

She covered her ears and went over her treasures in her mind. Something hard to part with, something precious. Her *Illustrated Legends of the Sea*? With her hidden notes? Her heart shrank. If it was that hard, it must be right. Only, what would the Rower do with a book about the Rower? If she had some of Kidcou's marvels from that glass island. Just one, a single one. Crystal glass in gold and pink and purple and —

There was a thump. A paper ball. It made one lazy bounce toward her and lay still. She waited. No light, no movement in Kidcou's window. She crept over and carefully scooped it up. It was her pebble, sent back with another message. She smoothed the crumpled sheet and held it up to the moonlight: *I didn't tell you because I was mad and wanted to show you. I took the note only because your dad shouldn't find it. I hided it to protect it. If you forgive me I tell you where it is. Kidcou*

He hadn't been asleep. Cheat.

I forgive you, she wrote back. *For now. Tell me where it is. But don't come down and pester me. Go to sleep. Stop spying on me or else I won't forgive you.*

She crept closer to Kidcou's window and threw the message back in, suddenly tense that he might change his mind. Where could he be hiding her note?

My grasshopfer guards it for you, the answer read. *Don't worry that I spy on you. I don't. I want to be your friend.*

Zelda humphed. She crept over to the terrace, making sure

to stay in the cover of the juniper hedge. After a moment of staring, she got it. She lifted the cage. The piece of paper, neatly folded, lay on the ground.

The chirping had stopped.

She suddenly felt sympathy for the insect in the cage. Maybe it wasn't so dumb after all to have a grasshopper as a pet. She plopped down in front of the cage the way Kidcou had, her note now tucked under her T-shirt. She spotted the grasshopper in the furthest corner of its prison. It sat motionless, in the shelter of a rolled-up leaf, trying perhaps to make her believe it, too, was a dry leaf.

"Don't worry, *hopfer*," she said."I won't harm you. Nothing can harm you in your awful cage."

She felt the folded paper tickle her belly when she moved. The grasshopper didn't stir. After a long moment, she noticed it carefully probing the air with its long antennae.

"Getting to know me, huh?" she said. "Soon you'll chirp and next you'll talk to me like to an old friend, won't you?"

The grasshopper didn't make a sound. Zelda wondered if she should stick a stalk of grass in for encouragement. She decided against it. A stalk might be a new scare. Poor critter, scared even in a cage.

"I won't harm you," she repeated. "Promise. Just scratch away on your cello and talk to me. What would you give the Rower if you were me?"

The grasshopper seemed to look straight at her with its huge eyes. Zelda couldn't tell if it was preparing an answer. Perhaps it was simply going to jump.

"Now, now, *hopfer*," she said. "Take heart. You're safe with me. Look, I will even open your door. That should prove it to

46

you, don't you think?" She slowly unlocked the wire gate.

"I am giving you a taste of freedom. But don't run away. I want to hear what you have to say."

She rested her head on her arm and waited.

"Gzzzgzzzgzzz," she heard, right from the cage.

Was it singing or was it talking? Was it talking in English or Italian? She lifted her head. The grasshopper had advanced to the middle of the cage. She placed her finger across the threshold of the gate. The grasshopper fell silent, moving its antennae up and down like grass in a breeze. It did not jump away. Perhaps the critter was special after all.

Zelda lowered her voice to a singsong:

"Grasshopper, talk to me,
show me a treasure, please."

The chirping set in again. They were talking to each other. That grasshopper must be very lonely in its cage. Only Kidcou came by from time to time for company. How could that make up for the long days and nights of prison? Solitary confinement, it was called.

Zelda felt the relief of the door being open, air passing through with a promise. It wasn't fair to live like that.

"Poor critter, do you want to be free,
do you want to come out and play with me?"

She moved her finger further into the cage. The grasshopper made a sudden leap and landed right at the gate.

"Climb on my finger and stay with me,
I'll put you in my cherry tree ... "

The moment she sang the words, Zelda realized how the grasshopper could be free and safe at the same time. She knew who would protect the creature. Especially if she herself set it down in the exact spot where her note to the Rower had been. She closed her eyes with the onrush of excitement. Yes, in the cherry tree. The grasshopper would fiddle and the Rower would know that Zelda had fulfilled her promise.

And Kidcou? Zelda knew it was unfair. She was taking his special friend, the one thing he had brought with him, the gift from Uncle Carlo. But she alone could do what Kidcou wouldn't dare. He was too scared to free the grasshopper. He hadn't chosen to come here. He had been sent. He couldn't imagine breaking out. But she, Zelda, knew all about it. She always found a way out.

"Grasshopper, I will set you free,
come out, come out and you will see."

As though it had understood and didn't care about her singing off-key, the grasshopper made a few steps and climbed up her finger. Zelda crinkled her nose at the prickly sensation. Now they were very close, facing each other. The grasshopper had cocked its head with curiosity, it seemed, as though it wanted to hear what else Zelda had to say.

"Come into my cherry tree,
you'll be safe and you'll be free.
Grasshopper, grasshopper,
take me to Italy."

She pulled her finger with its rider inch by inch through the door of the cage. She couldn't believe how big those eyes were, now that they were coming even closer. They seemed to be growing at a rate that made her dizzy. She felt with terror that she was getting lost in those eyes that didn't have a center.

The grasshopper was growing. Or was she shrinking? Her

body seemed to be falling away, weightless, to be lifted in the air by the curious gaze that wouldn't let go of her. She tried to scream but the rushing of a strong wind pressed the scream back into her throat.

Then, with a bump, the vertigo stopped. She found herself back on her branch in the cherry tree.

CHAPTER 6

"*Gzzz...Grazie*," said a grating, strangely vibrating voice next to Zelda.

Zelda barely managed to hold on to the tree.

On a branch beside her sat a person clutching something like a large violin case. Her mind slipped out of balance, but she stayed upright, squinting as hard as she could.

"You seem surprizzzed," she heard the grating voice again. "You called me up, as you may remember?"

She refused to look. "I'm dizzy."

"Ah dizzzy, tizzzy, quizzzical... Interesting words of the English language."

"So you do speak English?" Zelda forgot not to look.

"Any language. I take it in with the breezzze, so to speak, wherever I travel. I have traveled a lot, I dare say. Excuzzze me." The person sneezed and dusted off a long travel coat. "Consequence of life in a cage."

"Don't say you are really the grasshopper?!"

Zelda took in as much as she could in a few peeks. The pointed smile, the strangely huge sloe-eyes behind small glasses. Kidcou called his grasshopper "he." But this person crossed her legs as though to call them to Zelda's attention. Long, very long, thin legs in sand-colored pants. Laced boots with a heel. The Grasshopper was a she. She was sitting in a leisurely position, as if the branch were an armchair. As if she had spent her life in a tree.

"But how did you —?" Zelda was looking for a word that would fit.

"I may as well admit I have been waiting for this," the Grasshopper cocked her head at Zelda. "There is a certain limitation to the *conditio animalis* — life bound to the ground, if you know what I mean. Excuse me —" She sneezed again. "Perhaps we should ask how *you* did it?"

"I?" Zelda felt thrown off balance again by the proposition that this, whatever it was, was her doing. There must be some unthinkable mistake.

"Not I," Zelda protested.

"I see. You are suspecting someone else." The Grasshopper seemed to peer at her over the rim of her glasses.

Zelda realized that she suspected someone, indeed. But she wasn't going to believe anything too soon.

"What's this?" She moved one finger away from her branch to point to the case the Grasshopper was clutching.

"You will be surprised again. It's my cello."

Zelda took a breath. "That small?"

"A child's, to be precise. With only one string — which is enough for my music, you will understand."

Was the Grasshopper poking fun at her? Her mouth was pointed as though holding back a smile. Her eyes seemed to peek all around the shield of her glasses. Either her eyes or her glasses had to be the wrong size.

She set the cello case down in a fork of branches. Then she pulled a white handkerchief out from under her travel coat, shook the dust off and began to wipe her glasses. She wiped, tried them on, then started over. Each time she put her glasses back on, she seemed to focus her gaze on Zelda. Zelda wondered whether the Grasshopper had trouble seeing her, but the Grasshopper's intent gaze seemed to ask whether Zelda had trouble seeing.

Zelda watched the glasses disappear and reappear from the folds of the handkerchief. They stood out against the white cloth. A dark oval rim. Little ends of thread, where the legs were attached.

"Are you Uncle Carlo?" She managed to whisper. "Are you dead?"

The Grasshopper chuckled. It sounded like the rustle of dry leaves.

"My dear friend Carlo is quite dead indeed. Of course, he did not need his glasses any more, seeing clearly enough where he was going. We had much the same vision, I dare say. He passed them on, as you so well recognized."

"But, but how —?" Zelda almost forgot to hold on to the tree.

"I was passed on as he passed on, if you permit a bit of a poetic license between friends." Again, the chuckle of leaves.

"Don't you miss him?" Zelda frowned. "Kidcou misses him. He liked him!"

"Death, my dear, changes forms, makes some things heavy —hummingbirds, to quote an obvious example — and lightens others. Changing forms can be quite mesmerizzzing, dizzzying..."

Her grating, buzzing speech was a music Zelda had never heard before. What on earth was the Grasshopper talking about?

"How else could Carlo have made your little blond friend carry me with him? Hmm?"

"He made you?" Zelda bumped back to her senses. "He was your friend, but he put you in a cage for Kidcou?"

"Let's say, I had to travel in disguise."

"But Kidcou had no idea! Nobody told him. And he would never have figured it out. Not he. How can a friend do that?"

"It happened to serve our purpose rather well, you see."

"But he would have left you in your cage. Forever! Was that the purpose? And you find that fair?" She stopped herself. Was she already defending this creature? Fending for some Ms. Grasshopper?

Her tree companion cocked her head, pointing her smile. "I wish dear Carlo could hear you. You have the fine sense of justice of those for whom justice is not their daily bread, if I am not mistaken. May I ask you what your purpose is?"

Zelda felt strangely recognized. She took one hand off the tree and laid it on her belly as though to swear on the note hidden there.

"I promised you to the Rower, my ally. I knew the Rower would protect you if I opened the cage."

"The Rower, I see." The Grasshopper cocked her smile in the other direction. She seemed to be following perfectly.

"You *are* the grasshopper, aren't you?"

"Let's say, I was what I am not."

"Then Uncle Carlo was a grasshopper, too?" Zelda wasn't too proud of that question. She remembered what Kidcou had told her about his uncle. Would a boat come to bury a grasshopper?

"You have a fine quizzzical mind, *carina*."

"Carina?" Zelda crinkled her nose. "My name is Zelda! What's yours?"

"Why don't you call me what you called me before?"

"Called you?"

The Grasshopper's gaze encouraged her.

"Oh, when I got you out of that cage? That was hard work, I tell you."

"Hard work well done. Therefore, let me ask you again: What is your purpose?"

It sounded very important. Zelda had to squint for a moment.

"To free you, of course. What Kidcou could never have done. He's scared of everything. He's a goody two-shoes!"

The Grasshopper's gaze wandered down to Zelda's dangling feet. "Good in each shoe? Too good to be true?"

"He's a pest," Zelda confirmed. "Let's get out of here."

"Ah. Whenever you are ready." The Grasshopper made a little bow to her.

"I'm ready."

"For a long journey? Grasshoppers rarely make little leaps, you must know. Are you prepared?"

"How will I leap with you? I just twisted my ankle."

"We will travel while you sleep. Nothing will be easier."

"Let's take something to eat. I always get hungry when my mom takes us for a trip."

"Everything necessary is in my cello case." The long fingers tapped against it. "There is also room for you to sleep, you will see."

"I? Fit in there?"

"A perfect fit for anyone not much older than eight years."

Zelda squinted hard to remember she wasn't dreaming. She had been waiting all along for this to happen. She had been right to be eight years old and never a day older.

"We will get there fast," the Grasshopper said.

"Get where?"

"Is there anybody you would like to say good-bye to?"

"Get where?"

"Why, to Italy."

It took Zelda a moment to catch her breath. "To the glass island, you mean?"

"As you wish. To Italy."

Zelda searched in the strange, slanted eyes. She suddenly saw herself in a boat, far ahead of Kidcou. The Rower was guiding her to the treasure. But what about Kidcou?

"Kidcou can't keep anything he finds," Zelda felt a need to explain. "He loses everything."

"You, I understand, would not let that happen. He has nothing left then?"

Zelda stared at her for a moment. "Why don't you put another grasshopper in the cage? That way, he'll never know —"

"That you are missing, Zzzelda?"

"He won't miss me." She knew that wasn't true. "Okay, but he'll still have a grasshopper to talk to. And he can have my mother all to himself."

"The cage, I am afraid, will make our travel easier for both of us. Otherwise it might be hard for you, for any human, to keep up with me." The Grasshopper shifted her long, very long legs.

"You would jump away and leave me alone?"

"This is how we travel, leaping by yards and years. You are familiar with leap years, I imagine? But have you ever heard of anyone chasing after and catching up with a leap year?

You see what I mean. Your little blond friend is perhaps a bit ... hezzzitant, but he was wise enough not to lose me."

"He has lost you now. But how could you ever have been freed? Anyway, I told you, he always loses his stuff. But what if I can't keep up with you?"

"It's eazzzy. Whenever I turn back into a grasshopper," she lifted her large collar as though preparing to disappear into her travel coat, "you will find me in my cage. All you need to do is call me up again when you want us to converse, or traverse, or reverse."

"You mean, when I want to come back? Perhaps I don't want to come back."

"Ah. In that case, your little friend might set out with a search party, I suppose — unless you tell him where you are going and explain your purpose."

Zelda reminded herself that it was better not to leave things up for grabs, like messages in a tree. "But I won't say where," she warned as she slipped down.

The Grasshopper accompanied her with a wave of her long, very long hands as though directing an orchestra.

Zelda stuck her newly-penciled note back onto the branch where Kidcou had first found it.

I'm gone, it read, *because I set the grasshopper free. The critter is not what you think. But don't pester and come after us. It's important; it's for a purpose.*

P.S. Don't say a word to anybody. Do as I say or I'll never tell you the grasshopper's secret.

PART II

INTO THE PAST

CHAPTER 7

"Where are we?" Zelda asked the Grasshopper. She had never seen a cobbled street. The houses on each side looked like old doll houses that had received a few kicks too many.

"Where are we?" she asked again.

It was winter. People were huddling along in coats with large, raised collars. Some were wrapped entirely in fur. Others looked shaggy, freezing. A beggar under a gable was sticking his red hands and forearms out into the stream of passersby. A woman and five kids, bundled up in wool hats and scarfs, were pushing a huge pine tree along on a cart. A group of boys came running down a side street, their laced boots cracking up a storm on the stones. Their long, dark blue scarves were flying, and they all wore dark blue jackets and short pants. They were laughing and shouting and didn't seem at all cold. Zelda liked watching them run with their naked legs. She hardly noticed that they had entered a church with many pointed towers.

Now they were inside. She too, must be inside then, she realized.

She saw the boys race up a spiral staircase to a sort of balcony with a large organ, and now she, too, was on that balcony. There was no time to think about how she had got there.

The boys had thrown off their jackets and scarves. They were bombarding each other with paper balls, booklets, gloves, kicking chairs over. They were almost all blond boys. One boy was particularly fast at catching and returning the objects aimed at him even though he was among the smallest. Zelda grinned at the way he snatched a book hurled across the balcony just before it would have hit the belly of a man who had appeared at the top of the staircase.

She marveled at the speed with which they all lined up in orderly rows in front of the fat little man who had positioned himself at a raised lectern. He made an announcement in a language that sounded as though he had a bad throat. At his signal, they all began to sing.

"Aahh-ayy-eee-ohh-ooo," they sang, their voices rising higher and higher until they sounded like a bunch of piping flutes. Then their song with only one word climbed down the same musical staircase, step by step. These boys loved singing and they knew how to hold a note, Zelda noted.

They also clearly loved their fat little master who wiped his forehead with a handkerchief and pointed his stick at them. They eagerly followed his every command. At another of his announcements, they all turned the pages of their booklets with the rustle of a hundred birds taking off. The song they didn't know by heart had a strangely woven, sad melody. The boy who had caught the book in mid-air sang a solo. Perhaps they weren't real boys?, Zelda wondered. She must be hearing an angel.

"What's he saying?" She was suddenly aware that the Grasshopper was in the church, too, sitting right next to her.

"The song tells about Mary and Joseph on a mountainside, trying to rock their baby in the cold wind," the Grasshopper translated.

63

Up and down the song wove its sadness. Zelda recognized one word, "Ach!," a word her mother used when she got bad news. She was relieved when the choir and the soloist began a new song.

"What's this one about?"

"It is about a rose coming into bloom in the middle of winter," the Grasshopper said.

Zelda peeked at her companion. Roses bloomed in her father's garden all year long, but would anybody sing about it? Her father might, she had to admit, when he was in one of his good moods.

The soloist was so small they had put him on a footstool in front. His hair was cut in the same perfect square as most of the boys', a neat line of very short bangs crossing his forehead. The sides came straight down his temples, too long for a boy. Or was it a girl? All the others were boys, so he must be one, too.

There was something disturbing in his face. He seemed to be adoring someone or something only he could see. While he sang, the other boys appeared to be holding their breath as if caught in some spell. Then, at an energetic sweep of their master's arm, they all came back to life and finished in chorus. The master knocked on his lectern, gave the soloist's head a pat and stepped down, wiping his forehead and shouting orders of some kind.

The minute he disappeared from view, the boys fell to chasing and boxing each other as they had before. The little soloist was a favorite target of a group of older boys who tried to pin him down and tickle him. Zelda watched him wiggle himself free and thumb his nose at them. With a leap, he was back on his footstool just as the master reappeared. He marked his perfect timing with a laugh to himself, throwing his head back, his nose crinkled, his blond bangs stiff in the air.

"Kidcou??" Zelda squinted hard. "Is that Kidcou?"

He looked about half his age, with his weird haircut and big round cheeks, a real baby. And yet, once the link was made, there could be no doubt.

"Grasshopper, did you take him, too?"

She read the Grasshopper's amused smile.

"He's not following us, is he?"

But she knew that this Kidcou hadn't come along. The boy she knew wasn't here. She herself perhaps wasn't here. Her head was spinning. Nobody had turned around or stopped singing when she'd shouted out his name.

"Where are we?" She felt nauseated, the way she had on the cherry tree. She almost grabbed the Grasshopper's sleeve. "Are we really here? Is this ... Italy?"

"Just a leap or two from Italy," the Grasshopper replied, her fine long hand marking the rhythm of a new song the choir had begun. "We are in Vienna. A leap backwards in time, you understand. Your little friend here has barely entered the third grade. Listen to them. They are rehearsing for a Christmas concert. The famous Vienna choir boyzzz ..."

Zelda recognized the melody of "Silent Night." She felt reassured by the familiarity of the song. Her family didn't do Christmas, but if she recognized that song, she must be here, wherever here was.

A leap backwards in time? If this Kidcou suddenly was several years younger, how old was she? She fought with another attack of nausea. Then it occurred to her that logically, her age couldn't have changed if she could remember what had happened recently. It all came to her in an instant: her punishment, Kidcou's betrayal, her escape with the Grasshopper. She hadn't changed. Only this Kidcou had.

Perhaps going backwards in time was like remembering something from before. Remembering perhaps was like being there. But how could she remember those boys and their master? Kidcou had never peeped a word about them. He had never sung like that. Could one remember something one didn't know to begin with?

She listened with curious ears to the song she recognized. It sounded perfect, but the little fat master wasn't satisfied. He huffed and even shook his handkerchief at the famous boys as though trying to chase flies. He had his tiny soloist sing a line and part of the choir repeat after him.

This Kidcou seemed to be the star of it all. It was hard to believe, like watching him play a character in a movie. But there was no movie screen and no projector. She was and wasn't in this church with the Grasshopper who was wearing her old, dusty travel coat and Uncle Carlo's glasses. She herself was still in her bermudas, not feeling the least bit cold.

And there was Kidcou, a Kidcou she didn't know at all. He was not only younger, he was altogether different. He clearly played an important role in this group of singing boys, small as he was. He knew how to put up a good fight, and he had the best voice. They all seemed proud of him. How had he been able to hide all this from her?

All of a sudden the rehearsal was interrupted. A priest came hurrying up the stairs, holding his habit up as one would a dress. He whispered with the master, and both kept glancing in turn at a piece of paper the priest had brought, and at Kidcou. The little fat man looked worried. He called Kidcou over to him, knelt down beside him and talked to him. Zelda saw Kidcou's face go blank. He looked down, his body suddenly limp. All life had gone out of him.

He made a small nod. He didn't look up again. He turned around and stiffly followed the priest who took Kidcou's dark blue scarf and jacket from a chair. While everyone watched in utter silence, the priest led Kidcou down the stairs. The echo of their steps disappeared in the creaking of the church door.

Now the boys were in a tumult, shouting and asking and protesting. Zelda would have given anything to join them. It made her mad not to understand the brief words the master said, before he knocked on his lectern with fury and called another boy up to the footstool in front.

"Why? Why did they take him away?" Zelda tugged at her companion's coat. "Will he come back?"

"He won't, alas. The telegram from his foster parents calls for his immediately joining them in another country."

"Just like that? Why? Can't they leave him alone?"

"Most parents don't leave their children alone, you may have noticed. They do what they consider best for them. Your little friend's foster parents believe that the Vienna boys choir will not provide a future for him."

"A future?"

"Kidcou's father was a musician, a gifted pianist. But he was unable to make a living, which caused a lot of grief to his family, you see. When he and his wife died, Kidcou was raised by relatives. From the start, his foster parents were eager to give him an education that would not only further his musical talents but also allow him to become a lawyer or diplomat…"

"Like his foster father who works for the rich," Zelda scowled.

The Grasshopper weighed her head. "Kidcou has changed places and countries with them before. I noticed that you noticed his reaction?"

Zelda balled her fist. "Not fair. I would have yelled and kicked until they let me stay."

The Grasshopper looked at her as if she had said something of unusual interest.

"His foster parents have arranged to spend some time with him over Christmas, in Germany, before sending him to a boys' school in England."

"But does he want to go?"

"He does not know it yet."

"A school for lawyers for the rich?"

"We will see…we will soon see, I suppose."

"See what? I don't want to go to a boys' school. I want to go to Italy!"

"Certainly, to Italy." The Grasshopper performed a little bow to Zelda. She raised her long, very long fingers as if they were antennae, sensing a breeze. "Before we set out, you and I, I asked you if you were ready to travel in the grasshoppers' way. Do you remember?

"When grasshoppers leap, do they know the exact spot where they will land? There is the wind, there is promise and danger. What grasshoppers know is to trust their sense of direction and follow their destiny."

"Can't we use a map?" Zelda was getting fidgety.

"There is no map for destiny. In order to get to Italy, where your little friend has brought me from, we will have to use him as our guide."

"He's not my friend. I wish you'd come to America on your own. Why use him, when they keep sending him around to stupid places?"

"I admit, a grasshopper's travel may seem a bit of a zzzig-zzzag to other species. But remember, we are travelling in the past. In order to keep our direction and get to our destination, leaping along a life already lived is the surest way. Take heart, Zzzelda: we are on our way. To Italy."

CHAPTER 8

There was the movement and rattle of a train, a long compartment with red-brown seats on each side. The seats faced each other in pairs, with a tray table in between and red-brown curtains at each side of the window. The people in the compartment looked much like the ones Zelda had seen in the street near the big church. They were not wearing their coats now, but the women were wearing hats.

She spotted Kidcou, far back on the left side, at the window. As soon as she saw him, he was suddenly closer, very close, as though she had run up to him. He was wearing the same blue scarf over a blue coat, and his short bangs were covered by a dark blue beret. Opposite him at the window, a taller boy in a red sweater and tie was sitting next to a woman in a nurse's uniform who was knitting. Kidcou was stiffly pressed into the corner of his seat, his hands in his pockets, his chin in his scarf.

"Why don't you take off your coat?" the knitting nurse asked Kidcou.

Zelda turned to the Grasshopper. Zelda had understood. This was English. English with a throaty accent and sharp little explosions at the end of the words.

The Grasshopper didn't stir. It was amazing how she could sit and observe without stirring, without asking questions, without getting irritated and shouting like Zelda's mother, without joking or singing like her father. How could they be one and the same, the traveler next to her and the grasshopper in Kidcou's cage?

Kidcou didn't react to the question addressed to him. The nurse nudged the taller boy.

"Mark, does he understand English? Are you sure? Explain to him that it's a long way to Hamburg. He will be hot."

The boy shrugged. His face said, *what a bore*. The nurse bent forward, pronouncing every word with little explosions, "I don't want you to get sick, you understand me?"

Kidcou barely nodded. He didn't budge. He kept watching the grey-white landscape from under his lashes. Or rather, he pretended. Zelda could tell what he was really watching. The other boy was driving a tiny yellow toy truck over the window pane. He, too, was secretly watching Kidcou. He was driving his truck closer and closer toward Kidcou's half of the window.

She scanned the compartment. It gave her a start to see the same brown suitcase with metal corners stored away in a net right below the ceiling. The Kidcou she knew was already on his way with the same suitcase. She tried to remember what else he had brought along when he arrived in America. She only remembered the grasshopper. Now that she and the grasshopper had taken off, he wouldn't even have that.

The boy with the tie was breathing on the pane, letting his truck draw lines and curves on the moist surface. Kidcou watched him.

"What a nice car you have there," the nurse commented. "Why don't you let your friend also play with it?"

The boy shot Kidcou a glance. "Because it's mine."

"It's surely yours. But it's much nicer to share, Mark. Remember your privilege, what your father told you. I mean, your family being what it is. Therefore, you ought to remember sharing. I am certain it would make Helmut very happy."

There was a silence. Kidcou looked embarrassed.

"Helmet!" Zelda cringed whenever she heard his real name. Everyone at school except his teachers called him Kits.

"My father doesn't let me drive his car," Mark said.

"That's quite different, and you know it. You two should make friends. It will be nice for you to have a friend in the choir."

"If he gets admitted. My choir only takes boys who commit themselves for two years. At the least."

Kidcou looked as if he wanted to disappear into his seat.

"They won't take him, will they?" Zelda asked.

Kidcou took something out of his coat pocket, turning it closely in front of his eyes. It was a piece of glass. A piece of his treasure? But he hadn't been to Italy yet. It was an ordinary glass marble, sea-green, with white and blue spirals inside.

The boy, Mark, was now kneeling in his seat, reaching over, driving his truck to the spot on the window ledge where Kidcou had rested his elbow. The yellow truck climbed up Kidcou's arm trying to get into his hand. One corner of Kidcou's mouth went up. He did not accept the offer. Instead, he lowered the marble onto the ledge and started rolling it toward the other boy's half of the window.

Mark drove his truck up for a meeting, nose-to-nose. Then the truck drove off the ledge and stopped in mid-air, directly below the marble. The marble dropped. It was a pretty picture to see the yellow truck gulp up the shiny load and proudly promenade it along the window.

The game started again. Each time, the marble had to drop further before it was caught by the truck. Each time, the boys grew more excited. The nurse nodded, pleased. The marble finally missed the truck, and both boys leapt from their seats to pursue it. Zelda felt she was one of three players in the game of kicking the little glass ball further and further down the compartment. The nurse put down her knitting and called Mark back from between the other travelers' legs.

"We can't find it," Mark shouted, plunging back under a seat. Before he reappeared, Zelda saw him slip the marble into his cuff.

"Where is it?" he asked when Kidcou emerged from behind a big travel bag that was blocking off the neighboring group of seats. "Don't you have it?"

Kidcou shook his head and dove down again.

"He lost it," Mark loudly announced to the nurse.

Zelda noticed how he enjoyed pretending to help Kidcou's search. He walked up to the people in their seats asking them eagerly, making sure they knew the exact size of the marble. Everyone bent down to peek under the seats; legs were lifted, bags removed. Zelda balled her fists as Mark joined the regretful head-shaking whenever Kidcou reemerged at a loss, his face red, his beret stuffed in his coat pocket.

"Dirty cheat!" she hissed. She was ready to leap.

The Grasshopper took Zelda's hand for a brief moment. She started. Nobody ever did this to her. Nobody except the boys on her baseball team. Her father had come to understand that she didn't like it. But every now and then he would put her through a surprise back rub. When her mother was really proud of her, she would give Zelda's cheek a quick pat. The Grasshopper's touch felt like being wrapped in a fine, cool, soothing leaf. The faintest rustle seemed to accompany it. It was odd. Zelda stayed in her seat, but she refused to unball her fists.

Kidcou had slumped back into his seat, his coat unbuttoned. His bangs were sweaty. He was close to tears.

"I am sure it has rolled off on a slant right into a crack this big," Mark declared, fingering his cuff.

The nurse gave him a look. "We will do a thorough search once we have arrived and everyone has got out," she announced with many decided explosions of sounds. "I don't imagine that there are cracks in the compartment. It will show up again. Courage, Helmut."

"Well, someone could have hidden it. In order to take it. Or to fool us," Mark contradicted.

She gave him a sharper look. "And who, do you suppose, is that someone?"

Mark inspected the wheels of his truck. Then he drew up a tired smile. "Why, Helmut of course."

The nurse stared at Kidcou who stared at the nurse. With one quick grip, Mark dove into Kidcou's coat pocket, pulled out his beret and produced the marble from it.

"I knew it all along. He only pretended," Mark proclaimed. "He's funny. He has funny games." He sat down again, indifferent to the disbelief in the nurse's face.

After a moment of speechlessness, Kidcou opened his mouth.

Mark cut him off. "Okay, okay. Let's say, he didn't notice when he shoved that thing in his pocket, with his beret." He leaned forward with a broad smile and boxed Kidcou's knee. "You're a tricky fellow, you know. Nobody can fool me. But you really got me going on this. Pheww!" He pretended to wipe sweat off his forehead. "Isn't he something? The whole compartment..." He shook his head, looking hard at Kidcou.

Zelda turned to the Grasshopper, furious. The Grasshopper bent forward in her seat. Her long, very long hand went out in front of her, calling Zelda's attention to the scene.

Zelda watched Kidcou's face turn from bewilderment and pain into a blush, an insecure grin of pride.

CHAPTER 9

The train had disappeared without a trace. Zelda remembered — or had she dreamt it? — she had been tired from traveling through the grey winter landscape. She had gone to sleep in the cello case. Now someone was singing. It sounded familiar. Was she back in that church? Had the Grasshopper leapt backwards and they were starting over again? She didn't want to look. She didn't want to follow Kidcou around. But the singing wouldn't stop.

There was a big room with a stage, filled with people, kids, babies. Everybody was dressed in a festive way. In a corner, a huge Christmas tree was loaded with toys, trumpeting angels, and angel hair. A group of serious-looking teenagers were playing their instruments on the stage. Two boys stood up front. One of the boys was Mark; the other was Kidcou. Both were wearing dark blue blazers and ties. Right at this moment, they were each turning a page on the music stands before them. The quick movement didn't stop their singing at breakneck speed.

Zelda squinted. They sounded so much alike that she couldn't tell them apart. How did they know who was singing what? It was like one and the same voice running up and down against itself in some overexcited way that annoyed her. There was roaring applause. Everyone in the room clapped and stomped.

People shouted, "Bravo!" Some kids shouted, "Mark! Helmut! Helmut! Mark!"

Zelda didn't like it. Mark was in the limelight. Kidcou kept glancing at him. He bowed when Mark did, looking pleased as punch. The student orchestra pushed their chairs back noisily, stood up and bowed. Most of them smiled as though they had done something wrong, awkwardly holding up their instruments like pieces of evidence. Only Mark seemed unflustered. He bowed with a slightly puzzled face that seemed to say, "Are you saying all this is because of me?" Zelda wished Kidcou would stop beaming like a pumpkin pie. Was this clapping and bowing going on forever? All of a sudden, Mark, his one arm up in salute, leapt off the stage. He was immediately surrounded by a bunch of boys.

Kidcou hesitated for a second as everyone got up. Zelda read his desire to imitate Mark and leap off the stage too, with his short legs. Fortunately, a man with a small white mustache approached from the crowd and rescued him with a bear lift. They were joined by a woman with a greying hairdo of rolls and combs, who wore spectacles on a gold chain. Zelda turned to ask about them, but the Grasshopper wasn't in sight. Even if they looked more like grandparents, they had to be his foster parents. The lawyer, of course, who worked for the rich.

The couple seemed pleased with Kidcou. They hadn't liked his performing with the singing boys in Vienna, but now they let him perform again, and they looked pleased — even though his father had been a failure as a musician. It was confusing. His head was patted, and he slipped his hand into the woman's for a moment.

A younger couple came up to them, and the man called out for Mark with a voice that made everybody turn their heads. Mark reluctantly left the circle of his admirers and strolled over to the little group. The man who had to be his father boxed his son's elbow so that Mark's hand flew from his pocket. Mark slicked back his hair, grinning as though this was a good joke, and shook hands with Kidcou's folks. His father kept a proud, controlling hand on his son's shoulder while everyone clearly complimented both boys. Zelda didn't understand a word and yet she had the sensation of perfectly following everything. It was odd. She wasn't sure she even wanted to follow. Mark had a lot to say and everyone smiled at him. Kidcou didn't say much, but the pumpkin pie was again beaming from every pore of him.

Suddenly everyone shook hands. Other people in the room kept doing the same, Zelda noticed. There was so much hand shaking going on that she wondered if secret messages were being passed along, especially as many hands, men's hands, tended to wander into their own pockets when it was done. Kidcou's too.

She saw Mark wait until his parents had just turned their backs. He boxed Kidcou's hand out of his pocket just as his father had, winked at him and was gone. Kidcou giggled, holding his elbow. He glanced up at his foster father who smiled into his mustache as though to say, "Now that's a boy!"

A little girl with a head of dark wisps appeared behind Kidcou and reached out to touch his wheat-blond hair. What did she think she was doing?

Something ate into the scene, like a burn in a film projector, swallowing Kidcou and the little girl. Soon nothing was left but the distant hum of the Grasshopper playing her cello.

Zelda found herself in a child's room. She could hear someone sobbing, but nobody was in the room. A white carousel horse with a red saddle stood silently in a corner. Puppets were piled up in a box behind a marionette theater. Nobody was sitting at the desk. The small blue couch under the window was empty apart from pillows and a ratty old teddy bear. In a corner, a poster showed a group of boys in white sailor shirts, all looking like Kidcou, singing.

A moment of terror struck her with the thought that the Grasshopper had left with Kidcou while she was now stuck in his room. If she were trapped here, would she have to become Kidcou and live his life?

She quickly looked down at herself. She was still wearing her bermudas, her T-shirt, her tennis shoes. She made sure she still had her wiry curls on her head. No need to panic, she told herself, this is just another place we've leapt to. Hopefully we won't stay here for long. The Grasshopper might be outside already, checking the wind.

She gave the room her mean-eyed stare to make it disappear. If she shut her eyes, the room was gone. If she blinked, there it was again. If she refused to look, the strange sobbing became louder and louder until she was certain it was right in front of her, and she had to scan the room again.

She noticed a silver frame with a photo between the crayons, books and toys on the desk. A man and a woman were smiling at her. They looked like brother and sister, blue-eyed, both wearing aviator caps and leather jackets with white scarves. The woman smiled into the camera; she seemed to adore whomever she was looking at. His mother. Zelda's lips said the words without a sound. He had never told her. His parents were pilots and he had his mother's eyes. They are dead, she said to herself. Both dead.

She jumped when the door to the room was flung open. Kidcou ran in and threw himself onto the blue sofa. Zelda ducked, then she remembered that she wasn't really in the room. The teddy bear tumbled off as Kidcou took cover under one of the pillows. That's what she had been hearing, Zelda realized. He had been somewhere, sobbing all this time.

What a crybaby he was. She hadn't even been eight when she learned to squint so hard her tears had almost burnt out. The first time she squinted at her mother that way, her mother had dropped the wooden spoon she'd just threatened Zelda with. "What does she think she's looking at?" she had shouted although nobody else was in the kitchen. "This girl just stares like a —, like a —"

Too bad her mother had kept to herself what that stare was like, but Zelda knew enough. Her mother never lifted that spoon again. The neighbor boys, too, noticed the difference. She didn't have to do much any more, just give them that look. "Watch it," they started warning each other, "she'll scratch out your eyes."

She gazed back at the picture. They had fallen down with their airplane. Of course. That's how they had died. They'd gone up without him, just the two of them. Leaving him behind. Not fair.

Three adults walked into the room, one of them the woman with the rolls and combs and the spectacles on a gold chain who had to be Kidcou's foster mother. She sat down on the sofa edge and rubbed his back.

"Shh, shh," she said. "Now, now."

His foster father nervously stroked his groomed white mustache, one arm crossed over his chest to support the other. A younger man with an aviator jacket over one shoulder leaned against the door frame looking on, a cigarette in the corner of his mouth, a shock of blond hair falling close to his eyes. Zelda drew a quick comparison with the photo on the desk. If he were Kidcou's father he wouldn't hang back in the door doing nothing.

There was a plaintive voice from under the pillow.

"My boy," said the foster father, "today is Saturday. Saturday is English day. I know you are upset, but go ahead and express yourself in proper English."

Zelda drew in her breath. She, too, more than anything wanted to hear proper English.

"Why? Why not me?" Kidcou wailed. His head came up from under the pillow. "All the other boys were invited. But not me. Not me." He banged his fist against the sofa. "He hates me!"

"You know that's not true, Helmut," his foster mother said.

"Why on earth would anybody hate him?" the man in the door asked.

"My dear boy," the foster father let go of his mustache. "Let me explain again: Mark is older than you. He invited boys his own age. That's only normal."

"Disappointing, of course," his foster mother added. "But you have to understand."

Zelda didn't understand. Nothing rang normal to her. Least of all that anyone would cry buckets over a cheat like Mark.

"But we did the concert together," Kidcou brought out. "And we trained each day together."

85

"Yes, the two of you certainly worked hard. Now that's a different matter, don't you see?"

"But everyone said how they liked Mark and me together. And Mark said he also liked it."

His foster father took it in. "The concert was indeed quite a success. Mark, I believe, never found a match before. That doesn't mean, however — "

"He said I could sing for him on his birthday!"

"That snake!" Zelda shrank back from her own shout. She expected them all to turn around and grab her like a spy.

There was no reaction. They had no idea that she was there.

She looked around for the Grasshopper, then shouted again into their silence, "SNAKE! CHEAT!"

"Well, it was a nice thing for Mark to say," his foster mother tried. "But perhaps it wasn't meant as — "

" — a real invitation," her husband filled in.

"Nice??" Zelda howled. "He was making a fool of him in the meanest way. Sing for me! Kiss my arm, that's the invitation, if you ask me." She wished they'd ask her.

"But why? Why?" Kidcou went into another sobbing spell.

"Just forget about him," his foster father ordered.

His wife stopped him on his way out with a gesture that made him pass her his big white handkerchief for Kidcou.

"I thought I ... was his friend," Kidcou said in a small voice.

"I'll tell you what," the younger man left the door frame to look for something on Kidcou's desk. "That guy isn't even worth your while." He extinguished his cigarette in Kidcou's painting palette. "You'll make lots of other friends here."

Kidcou's foster parents shot him looks of warning. He shrugged sheepishly. Kidcou was not going to stay and make friends,

Zelda knew. He was going to be sent to Italy.

"Listen, old man," the younger man picked up the framed photo for a second and put it back down. "Your uncle's got an idea for you."

Kidcou came out from under the pillow and blew his nose. His face was red and swollen. The man who was his uncle went down on one knee and playfully put his finger on Kidcou's forehead.

"I can tell there's something on your mind that's better than any old birthday party."

Kidcou's eyes showed the bluest hint of hope as his uncle wiggled his fingers like a magician to catch his thoughts.

"Ah! It's coming. The best thing in the world. You can't hide it from me. It speaks with a loud, clear voice. It says: *Marzipanbrote*! Am I right? Or — am I right?"

Zelda was at a loss. Marrtse punnbrowte? Whatever he was talking about, the round eyes and mouths of Kidcou's foster parents confirmed that his uncle had hit the mark.

"Can we hear it in English, too?" his foster father suggested.

"Marzipan breads," Kidcou translated for his uncle.

"How about a whole box of them? The biggest box you've ever seen? Shake your head for no, nod your head for yes. No? Yes? No? YES!" Kidcou's head followed his uncle's shaking and nodding. He looked like a rabbit in love with a magnificent snake.

"And how are we going to get this wonder of wonders? Well, we'll pull it right out of your ears. Don't move!" He put a fist to each of Kidcou's ears. Kidcou blinked as if ready for a miracle. His uncle pulled. He bulged his muscles, he groaned. And — bang! — his fist swung around. Kidcou stared cross-eyed at the blueish banknote in front of his face.

"Peter!" Kidcou's foster mother shook her head with a smile. Her husband shrugged.

Kidcou took the money from his uncle's fist. His uncle got up, blowing a shock of hair out of his eyes.

"Hard work," he smiled broadly. "We'll always work hard to make you happy, don't you know? Now run your bike over to the delicatessen and get yourself the biggest box of Lübecker Marzipan they've got."

Lew Baker?, Zelda puzzled. Marzipan breads from a baker named Lew? It was amazing how many treasures Kidcou got that she had never seen or even heard of.

"Wait for me!" she shouted as Kidcou jumped up and everyone left the room. "I want to see them. Grasshopper, where are you? Don't leave me alone in this room!"

CHAPTER 10

With a bump, Zelda landed outside, in the street. Or was it the bump of Kidcou's bike hitting the pavement? He seemed in a hurry, pedaling in a standing position to make up for his short legs, his wool scarf flying about his face. A big, flat, shining box on the luggage carrier stuck out on both sides. Was he already back with his bounty?

Kidcou leapt off his bicycle at the opposite sidewalk, parked the bike against a garden wall, and rang a bell at a cast-iron gate. His face was red, his breath was pushing eager little flags of mist toward the house behind the wall. He ripped a transparent wrapping from the box and took the cover off. Zelda hesitated a moment. She was sneaking up on him. She noticed the wet hair on his neck. She peeked.

"Wow!" escaped her. She leapt back, only to realize, once again, that she hadn't been noticed. The box was huge. Inside she saw row after row of neatly packed "loaves." They looked like solid, black, chocolate bars. Each was as long as her pinky but twice as thick, with smoothly rounded corners.

She could tell Kidcou was holding his breath. He peeked through the gate, quickly grabbed one of the breads and bit half of it off. Zelda saw that the chocolate was only a thick coating. Inside, what looked like moist dough, white as snowflakes, had to be the marzipan. Kidcou almost closed his eyes as he turned the second half around in his mouth.

Zelda licked her lips. She would have given anything to snatch one of the fat little breads out of the box while Kidcou wasn't watching. He rang the bell again, more determined this time. Zelda saw empty flower beds and high evergreen hedges hiding a brick house. She heard a door opening and expected his uncle or his foster parents to come out and applaud him and his box. Instead, an old woman, wrapped in a thick shawl, came shuffling up the path.

"Is Mark there?" Kidcou asked before the woman had reached the gate.

Zelda was dumbfounded. He had taken his treasure to Mark's house? The minute he'd got it?

"He can't come out right now. He is occupied," the old woman said.

"I am Helmut. His friend. We did the concert together." The woman's face was blank. "I live over there." Kidcou pointed up the street to make her understand. "Couldn't you call him?"

"I am afraid he is with his guests. He is celebrating his birthday."

"I know," Kidcou said, his eyes pleading. From the open door in the house came a waft of voices, laughter, shouts. The old woman looked at the box.

"Would you like me to convey a message perhaps?"

"Oh yes," Kidcou hurried. "I have something for him. I want to — I got all these marzipan breads and it's his birthday. I thought he likes them too —"

"No way!" Zelda cried out.

"I see. You would like to share your candy with him?" The old woman looked neither impressed nor pleased. Kidcou nodded. His eyes, bigger than ever, were fixed on her face.

The woman opened the gate and Kidcou made a step to walk in.

"Let's see now," the woman stopped Kidcou before he could enter the garden. "Perhaps — "

She lifted a corner of the white tray of marzipan breads. "Yes, there is another layer underneath. So I'll take this one, alright?"

Kidcou stared at the one empty space in the neat pattern of rows. He blushed, nodded. She lifted the tray out of the box.

"That's very lovely. Mark will be pleased." She turned to walk away.

"Wait!" Kidcou picked a marzipan bread from the remaining tray and plopped it into the gap.

"Very lovely," she repeated. They were contemplating the rows restored to their perfection. Almost perfection. Zelda saw the smudge of Kidcou's hot thumb on the one little loaf.

"Thank you. And now you will excuse me." The old woman pushed the gate back with her elbow, balancing the luscious tray on her hands and forearms. The gate clicked.

"Tell him it's from me. From Helmut," Kidcou shouted after her although she was only a step away.

"Don't worry, I'll tell him." She shuffled away faster than she had come.

Zelda squinted hard. Now there was only one layer left in the box, and it had a gap. She counted. Forty-seven. He had given away forty-eight loaves of Lew Baker's marzipan breads. For what?

Kidcou hadn't moved. He stared at the house, examined the forty-seven shiny black loaves in his box, stared at the house again, stepping from one leg to the other. He grabbed an iron bar of the gate with his free hand and shook it. Nobody came. His finger went tentatively back to the bell. He hesitated, then looked around as though feeling watched.

Zelda shrank back. He was looking right at her. His eyes were filled with hurt and shame. It was too late to look away; she saw he had hoped to pay for his way in. His bargain had been rejected.

She felt heat rising to her face. This was how he lost his treasures. He'd lost his parents, and the boys in the choir. Now he'd given away half of all he had left. His guilty turning around was his confession.

He looked up the street in panic. His foster parents and uncle had stepped out of their house a good block up the street, as if wondering where he might be. They were quite a distance away, but they had clearly spotted him. Kidcou quickly closed the box, popped it back on his bike and pedaled up the street, waving.

How long had they been standing there, watching? What had they seen?

"Well?" Kidcou's uncle asked when Kidcou jumped off his bike and lowered the kickstand. "Let's see that little box."

They passed the box back and forth between them, admiring its size and weight. Kidcou's gaze followed them with a strained smile.

"Happy?" his uncle asked.

"And how!" Kidcou assured him.

"Already opened, eh?" His uncle teased. "Let's see how many you've got." He lifted the cover.

"Take, take!" Kidcou shouted, jumping up and down. "There are so many!"

They laughed. "No way, old man. They are all for you, re-member?"

Kidcou nodded, flushing. He bent over the box and counted out loud the number of loaves. Zelda saw his foster parents exchange a look. She read regret in it, and pity. She wanted to punch them for having spied on him.

Kidcou let his uncle put the box back on his bike.

"And what do you say?" his foster mother reminded him.

"Thank you, thank you, Uncle Peter!" Kidcou leapt into his uncle's arms and buried his face in his leather jacket.

His uncle slapped Kidcou's back to send him along. "Have a great day, old man. And don't you worry about your supper!"

"Grasshopper!" Zelda called out. "I can't stand this."

"You are worried about your little friend?" Zelda hadn't expected a reaction, but her companion was there in her familiar travel coat, right next to her.

Zelda was speechless for a moment. Kidcou and everyone else had disappeared. The street was still there but looked frozen now, like a photograph.

"How do you know?" Zelda looked at her with suspicion. "You weren't watching with me. Why did you leave me alone?"

"You could not see me, Zzzelda. I was there in the room and in the street, just a small leap to the back. It is sometimes useful to observe things from a distance, you see, to get an overview."

Zelda thought it over for a moment. She frowned. "If you were there, couldn't you have stopped him from being so stupid? Giving away his uncle's gift! To his so-called friend." She pretended to puke.

"Alas. The offering was made and nothing was given in return.

The door was shut in his face. Is it stupid to have tried? What if his plan had worked, if the door had opened?"

"It would never have worked. Not with that cheat. And Kidcou didn't even say what he wanted to get with all these marzipan breads. He's a moonsheep. He's blind."

"Ah. The question we need to ask then is, can we see clearly when we are desperate for a friend?"

"I'd ten times rather not have a friend at all. Kidcou knew darn well he'd been tricked with that marble. 'Sing for him for his birthday!' Did you hear that? He's been so pompous and flattered by that snob."

"Seeing him pompous and flattered that way is quite annoying, you mean?"

"He bugs the ship out of me. I told you."

"Do you then suppose Mark was annoyed, too?"

Zelda's frown gave way to her mean-eyed stare. "Whose side are you on? Not on that cheat's?'

The Grasshopper's eyes seemed to raise themselves over the top of her glasses to inspect her.

"In order to understand what we see, it may help to see it from more than one side. Do you seizzze my meaning?" She rolled her eyes up and down, to the sides and even backwards.

Zelda couldn't help laughing. "Don't say you can see the back of your own head!"

"Try me," the Grasshopper answered with a smile.

There was a silence.

Zelda said, "Still. Why can't he see anything?"

"Let me tell you what I see in the back of your head while you are asking me. If you had been able to step in, you would have stopped your little friend. Isn't that what you are think-ing? You would have told him what you know about Mark, that he is anything but a friend. Yet you know it wouldn't have stopped him, isn't that true? He wouldn't have believed you, Zzzeldina."

Zelda gave her a grim look.

The Grasshopper slightly stooped down to her, enveloping Zelda with her gaze. "There are things we have to see with our own eyezzz to believe them."

CHAPTER 11

Zelda felt her stomach sink as if an elevator had taken off with her at great speed, without warning. When there was solid ground under her feet again she found herself at the end of a station platform. Here and there, porters were leaning on their luggage carriers. A huge clock at the head of the hall showed almost five o'clock. Right underneath it, near the end of the platform, a small figure was sitting on a suitcase.

The dark blue woolen jacket, the scarf, the beret? Kidcou again. Zelda's stomach settled. He must be setting out finally for Italy. Or had he already arrived? He was holding a placard with his name on his knees. Helmut Berghaus, she read.

Two trains arrived simultaneously, hissing and spitting vapor and screeching to a halt. Kidcou covered his ears. Boys of all ages and sizes, some as tall as men, spilled out from both trains. Suitcases and backpacks, bags with tennis rackets and hockey sticks were passed through windows and dragged along the platform. Some younger boys hung back, clutching the hands of adults. Others were running ahead to greet boys from the other train, anxious to leave their parents behind.

Now an announcement came over the station speakers, in English, with a funny accent. So much for Italy. Zelda cursed. This was the dreaded boys' school in England.

Little by little the tumultuous crowd formed a line toward

the exit hall. An adult who had to be a teacher was shouting about buses waiting to take the boys to the school.

Kidcou was watching with flushed cheeks. Some older boys stopped and stared down at him.

"One from the Lost and Found," one of them pointed at Kidcou's name sign.

His companion, a youth with a carrot-red crew cut, snatched the sign and held it behind his back as Kidcou rose in alarm.

"Give him a break," a third boy with a Sherlock Holmes cap pleaded. "He won't remember his name without it."

They roared, handing the sign back and forth between them, twisting their tongues over the name. Zelda couldn't help grinning at "Hell nut" and "Perk mouse."

"I'd never remember that name either," a bulky boy, with a sports bag over his shoulder, said and dropped the placard back into Kidcou's hands.

"You've got too much muscle to remember anything," the carrot-head sneered.

A mock boxing match ensued that slowed down the exiting line and quickly vanished as the teacher's head came into view. Kidcou followed them with his eyes, half in shock, half in admiration.

"And what about you?" The teacher cut into Kidcou's stare. "You don't want to miss the bus, do you?"

The platform was rapidly emptying.

"I — I will get fetched. By Mr. ... Mr. Bisser?"

"Mr. Bither. I see. I wonder why he's not here? Hm. Why don't you get into the bus? At school, you'll easily find out where you belong."

"I must wait, my foster father told me. I must."

"Very well, young man. Mr. Bither won't be long now."

Mr. Bither did not show up. Zelda saw Kidcou sink into a heap as the hands of the huge clock advanced past six o'clock. Every now and then he turned around, frantic, and scanned the whole station. A couple of porters came up to ask him what the matter was and he repeated that he had to wait to be fetched by Mr. Bither.

Zelda hated waiting. Why didn't he do something? She tried to call the Grasshopper up. She threw her head around every now and then, but the Grasshopper was nowhere to be seen. Why couldn't she make a leap on her own?

It was unfair. He kept his name sign straight on his knees and didn't move from the spot. She stomped. There was nothing she could do. Nothing but follow the hands of the big clock.

No other trains arrived. It was getting dark. After another anxious look at the clock, Kidcou put the placard on the floor and bent his head over his knees. Zelda squeezed her eyes shut, refusing to watch for another moment.

"Berghaus?" A voice made her jump with relief. "You better come along. Mr. Bither didn't make it."

Kidcou barely glanced up at the two tall boys in front of him. He bent over to pick up his name sign, quickly wiping his nose. Then he followed them, lugging along his brown suitcase with the metal corners as fast as he could.

Before Zelda could worry about keeping pace with them, the Grasshopper's next leap had spun her up again into a nausea, and deposited her in a room with a barred window. Pillows were sailing through the room, accompanied by giggles and shrieks. Three small boys in long nightshirts were gamboling over three iron beds. On the fourth, on top of the neat grey blanket, stood Kidcou's suitcase.

The door opened.

"Quiet, monkeys," a voice cut into the tumult. "The zoo is closed. In your beds."

The voice was followed by a youth strutting into the room, his hands in his pockets. Zelda recognized him in an instant as the carrot-head who had snatched Kidcou's name sign. He went through the room as though on a stroll. The three youngsters tried to sit still on their beds and control their giggles. The carrot-head snatched a sock from under one bed and shoved it into the nose of the boy sitting above.

"Greetings from the cheese department," he announced.

The boys turned red in their effort not to sputter. With the same rapidity a comic book was pulled from under one of the grey blankets. The owner's mouth went down as he watched his book disappear into the pocket of the carrot-head whose face stayed indifferent. He stopped in front of Kidcou's bed. His sharp grey eyes seemed to pierce holes into the suitcase.

"Right." He turned to them so suddenly that one of the boys jumped. "Your new roommate has arrived. Helmut Berghaus. Not exactly an English name, as any baboon might realize. Or do you, Riley?" He balled his fist under one boy's chin. The boy froze.

Another tall youth came strolling in, pretty-faced, with dark wet curls and a snub nose. The carrot-head turned to him. "The zoo has been invaded by the German enemy. Not one of the tough kind, however. Got lost at the station, holding on to a name card." He gave the pretty snubnose a grin that was eagerly returned. "Not much of a name anyway, Burkhouse. Or was it Burphouse?"

"Burphouse! Burphouse!" The small boys were almost thrown off their beds with glee. The pretty snubnose, too, was doubled over.

"Shut your trap, baboons. There's nothing funny about enemy invasion. You'll soon find out, and it'll be too late. Let's have a look at what he has to hide." He winked the snubnose over to open Kidcou's suitcase.

"Tsk, tsk, a mama's boy." The snubnose handed the head boy the photo in the silver frame that Zelda had seen on Kidcou's desk. The three roommates twisted their necks to get a peek.

"Not a pretty picture. I told you. And look at this." The carrot-head pulled the poster with the famous choir boys from a cardboard roll and showed it around. "Mama's singing boy. Of course," he nudged the snubnose. "Bither mentioned it. A music scholarship. Mama and Papa don't have the money it takes. Note that, baboons. That's the only way an enemy could steal in."

"Cheap trick," the snubnose confirmed, rolling up the poster as though he might dirty his fingers.

"But they think they are better than anyone else because they sail in on a scholarship," the carrot-head continued his search. "The specially gifted! Like the piano star who couldn't kick a ball. Remember that, monkeys? This one, too, will need toughening up."

He pulled something from the very bottom of the suitcase and held it up like a trophy. It was Kidcou's ratty teddy bear.

"You need a little comfort at night, Durham?" He stuffed the bear under the sheet of one of the boys. Its owner shrieked and kicked the bear over to the next boy's bed where another shriek and kick made it land on the floor. "I'll trust you guys will help him shape up. No sissies in the zoo."

"He's coming," the snubnose warned from the door. "With Bither."

The carrot-head knocked down the cover of the suitcase. He leaned against the iron bars of the bed, his arms crossed over his chest.

Kidcou came in, still wearing his jacket, his beret stuck into a pocket. He was flanked by a tired-faced, bald man in a tweed jacket who introduced him to his roommates and ordered the youngster called Durham to show him the washrooms before lights-out. He presented the carrot-head as Snyder, the head boy, and the snubnose as his assistant, Brown.

"They'll instruct you about all the rules," he said. "If there's any trouble just turn to them."

Zelda saw that Kidcou flinched when he recognized the carrot-head from the station. He stole glances at his suitcase with its open locks while Mr. Bither was talking. Finally his gaze fell on his teddy bear on the floor.

"Let's give your new roommate a proper welcome, monkeys," the carrot-head commanded once Mr. Bither had left. "And with the proper pronunciation," he added with a wink. "One, two, three — "

"How do you do, Burphouse," the boys intoned in chorus and burst out laughing.

Kidcou looked confused. He pressed his lips into a smile.

"So, they rescued you from the Lost and Found, after all. Couldn't find your way by yourself, hm? Preferred to sit there and snivel."

Kidcou shot him a glance of embarrassed surprise.

"Ah, you wonder how I know, don't you? Tell him, Brown."

The snubnose took over in a nasal lecture. "Nothing here stays hidden. That's the supreme rule. Big Brother is watching you all the time."

"The law of the jungle. Isn't that so, baboons?"

The boys busily nodded. Kidcou watched them, his head bent, from under his lashes. He hadn't moved from the spot near the door through which he had entered.

"Let's start with a few lessons then, shall we? Number one: Life is hard for a crybaby. Notice that, all of you. Number two: Keep your suitcase closed. Things might fall out that you'd rather not show around. Things like, let's see ... a doll. Or a baby bottle. Get my point?"

Kidcou stared at him, stunned. His roommates got it. They signaled each other. The head boy's voice whipped them back to attention:

"Why don't you close your suitcase properly, Burkhouse? And pick up what you dropped?"

Everyone's eyes wandered from Kidcou to the spot on the floor where his teddy bear had landed, and back to him. Two red patches appeared on Kidcou's cheeks. He didn't move.

"I didn't," he brought out with only the slightest tremor in his voice. "I didn't drop."

"He didn't drop!" the head boy broke through the general merriment. "I'll drop dead. The crybaby is funny. Well, if he didn't, it can't be his, right? So why don't you do us a favor, Burkhouse, and drop that ugly, ridiculous thing there out of the window?"

Kidcou seemed glued to his spot near the door, at a somewhat safe distance from everyone.

"Well? We are waiting. Or shall I ask one of your roommates

to throw it out?"

None of the boys looked keen on carrying out the task.

The red of Kidcou's cheeks had spread to his ears. He lowered his head, his lips pressed together. All of a sudden he stomped forward like a small bull. He crossed the passage between the beds, scooped up his bear, swung it around and, in the same motion, stuffed it in his suitcase. He stepped back just enough to be out of reach, before he gave the head boy a pouting, defiant glance.

"Bravo. Let's give your new roommate the applause he deserves," the carrot-head smirked.

"Yeah! Yeah!" the boys clapped and shouted with relief.

"Admitting to be a mama's boy is the first step toward becoming a man — hopefully." He measured Kidcou, one eyebrow raised. "It's an honor to be at this school, you understand? You didn't pay for it, Burkhouse. Therefore you'll have to qualify. And as you've been such a good boy just now, I'll give you permission to qualify."

The pretty snubnose rubbed his hands.

"You are going to show us your qualification by singing us a lullaby. Right now."

Kidcou stared at him, his mouth open in disbelief.

"Ah. The bird's already opened its beak ... "

"Let's hear a pretty song," the snubnose chimed in.

"I'm listening." The head boy turned his head sideways, one hand behind his ear.

There wasn't a sound in the room.

"What?" The piercing grey eyes shot toward Kidcou who stepped back as though struck.

Zelda felt ready to leap in and scratch out those eyes.

"Can a mama's boy be a pighead at the same time? I ask you, baboons, is that possible?" The boys shook their heads, entranced by the confrontation. "That's right. There's no room here for pigheads." The head boy uncrossed his arms. His elbows wide, fists on his hips, he made a step toward Kidcou. "Do what I tell you," he threatened, coming closer.

"No way!" Zelda shouted. But she knew it was useless. Nobody heard her.

Kidcou receded. Zelda saw sweat on his face. The carrot-head slowly reached out. Kidcou bumped into the wall. The grip went to his jacket right below his throat and pinned him to the wall.

"Sing, I tell you."

"No!" Zelda screamed. "Don't!"

Kidcou looked at the grey eyes in terror. Zelda pummeled her ears with her fists as Kidcou's mouth opened, trying to force a sound.

"Ah, it's coming," the carrot-head relaxed his grip and stepped aside expectantly. "Keep trying, mama's boy."

One of Kidcou's roommates had opened his mouth as though in an effort to help Kidcou along. Another one was biting his nails.

"Don't, Kidcou," Zelda pleaded.

Kidcou's eyes narrowed. A flash of the brightest hatred escaped before he squeezed them shut. The effort of gathering all the breath at his command made his shoulders rise. His elbows drew up at his sides. For a moment he hovered like a marionette caught in a soundless scream. Then the marionette howled out a piercing, plaintive, "Quaaak!"

The carrot-head stepped backwards in surprise. He looked disgusted.

"Quaaak! Quaaak!" Kidcou went, his elbows going up and down in rhythm.

He seemed to be imitating the position his torturer had taken just a moment ago. Zelda couldn't bear to think what would happen next. Stuck in his spot, Kidcou was waddling from one foot to the other, quacking away, flapping his elbows like a crazy duck.

The pretty snubnose couldn't help bursting out laughing. The carrot-head looked around and shrugged. The smaller boys hesitated only one second, then they became hysterical.

"Quaaak! Quaaak!" they joined in, leaping from their beds and imitating the duck walk.

"What the devil is going on here?" A grey-stubbled head appeared in the door.

Everyone stopped on the spot.

"The zoo got a new member, I'm afraid. Burkhouse, a duck," the head boy pointed to Kidcou. Zelda saw that he couldn't hide his anger even though he tried. "We'll cage the duck in time. Nothing to worry about, Prof." He went toward the door. "Brown, why don't you get them ready for lights-out?"

With perfect cool, his hands in his pockets, he left the room.

CHAPTER 12

Zelda sat up with alarm. Had she fallen asleep? The carrot-head, the boys in their nightshirts, everyone was gone. She had not felt the Grasshopper's leap, and now she had missed the best of it, Kidcou and his roommates enjoying his victory over the head boy. There were only adults in a room with a huge desk and heavy brown leather chairs.

The room was stuffed with books. There was an old painting of a deer hunt, and she recognized a photo of the queen of England. A man with a white beard and eyebrows like her father's was sitting behind the desk talking to a man with sad, drooping eyes. They were talking about something she didn't understand even though she understood the words: scholarship, patrons, diplomacy. She kicked the empty air with her foot. This still wasn't Italy.

"Grasshopper!" she shouted into the room.

There was a knock on the door. A young man with dark-rimmed glasses peeked in. He nervously shook a strand of hair off his glasses as he entered, his hand gently prodding Kidcou into the room with him. Zelda snorted. At least he hadn't got to Italy without her.

Kidcou was dressed in a navy V-neck sweater and tie. His hair was combed with water. He looked thinner and even more pale than when Zelda had seen him last. He listened to the man with the white mustache who assured him that he, the headmaster, could be trusted. He invited Kidcou to tell him his troubles, and then didn't wait to listen. He spoke about honor, scholarships, the school tradition.

Zelda wondered what the point was. She could tell Kidcou was scared, trying hard not to let on. He shrunk when the headmaster lifted a record from his desk and held it up for him. It was a record of the famous choir boys. The cover showed them dressed in white monk's habits in a chapel. Big golden letters across the top read, "Silent Night."

"You have had some good, peaceful time to think this over, Berghaus. I am sure you are ready now. Why don't you sing us one of these songs that you know so well?" The headmaster sounded upbeat. "Any one of them." He looked at the young man with the glasses who blinked nervously.

The young man went down on one knee to whisper a word into Kidcou's ear. He whipped a silver tuning-fork from his pocket, tapped it briefly against his finger, held it to his ear, and hummed a note. Then he took a demonstrative breath, lifted his hand, and mouthed the first words of the song. Kidcou had followed him with great concentration. He, too, had taken a deep breath, opened his mouth, and now closed his eyes in the effort.

"Quaaak, quaaak," came out.

Zelda slapped her thigh. Seeing Kidcou in such an act of rebellion was something beyond her wildest imagination. He was even more daring than he had been with the carrot-head. This Kidcou had nothing in common with the one she knew. This one was a daredevil. He obviously didn't want to stay at this school; he wanted to get out of there.

The music teacher threw his strand of hair off his glasses. The headmaster looked at the man with the drooping eyes who nodded for him to proceed.

"You can't fool us, Berghaus." The headmaster drummed his knuckles on the desk. "I don't have to play your own record for you to prove how well you can sing that song. And you know we all know it. There's no reason to be shy and hide the fact. Don't you agree?" Kidcou nodded earnestly. "You see, we have thought out a lovely role for you at our school. A role that will be very much to your liking: lots of musical studies, concerts, performances. You are free to take it, Berghaus. It's yours. All you need to do in return, is let us freely enjoy your singing. Do you understand me?"

"Yes, Sir," Kidcou said.

"Excellent. Let's try it again." He stopped drumming on his desk and gave a signal.

The music teacher whispered into Kidcou's ear again, struck his fork, and he and Kidcou took breath together.

"Si-hi-lent night," the teacher's voice took the lead.

"Quaaak, quaaak," Kidcou joined in.

Zelda slapped her thigh again with glee. Kidcou's way of defying authority was a dream. He himself, however, looked like a nightmare. His face was grey; his body seemed limp as if all life had gone out of him. This was how he had looked in the church in Vienna when the telegram arrived.

The music teacher wiped his forehead. The strand of hair fell back over his glasses as he rose up. The headmaster reverted to his drumming. His beard went up and down as though he was munching on words he chose not to say. The man with the drooping eyes raised his eyebrows.

Kidcou looked at them with a blank face, waiting. With a wave of the headmaster's hand, he was dismissed. The music teacher prodded him out of the room.

"I told him not to sing," Zelda said into the silence. She turned to the Grasshopper who wasn't there. "He didn't give in. He beat out that red-headed rat. He must have heard me. He even managed mean-eyes. I can't believe how he did it.

"But now he goes on and on. Why not just say, I hate this school and I won't stay and I won't sing? Why does he keep trying? I know they think he's mocking them. They won't let him make a fool of the headmaster. They'll get him, Grasshopper. Couldn't we do something? I don't want to watch this."

There was no reaction, no reply. In front of her, in the room, the headmaster and his droopy-eyed companion all of a sudden looked groomed and polished like shoes for Sunday. She followed the direction of their equally polished gazes. Kidcou's foster parents were sitting on the other side of the big desk. How had they suddenly turned up? She hadn't even gone through the queasy elevator movement. But there they were, in the same room, looking irritated. Zelda guessed what their presence meant.

"We would certainly like to, but at this point, I am afraid, we are unable to reconsider," the headmaster declared with a thick layer of regret. "As Dr. Wright has explained in his letter," he nodded to the man with the drooping eyes, "we have carefully observed young Helmut for several weeks. We find that his state of refusal — "

"We have never seen him in such a state," his foster father cut in. "Helmut has never been rebellious. His success in Vienna quite proves the contrary, I would think. I don't understand how this —"

"— is not intentional," the headmaster continued, nodding as if he perfectly agreed. "Dr. Wright is convinced it is not in Helmut's control at this point. We are aware of his situation: a new country, a new language, a new school. We have no doubt about the giftedness of your foster son. It is amply documented, of course, and was the reason for his scholarship.

"Why don't we wait a semester or two and, in the meantime, give young Helmut a chance to catch his breath, so to speak?" He looked around expectantly.

"Truly, I don't see how we could wait," Kidcou's foster mother twisted the gold chain of her glasses with nervous fingers, "with my husband being sent to Turkey in June ... "

"Our hands are tied," her husband joined her. "We thought everything had been perfectly prepared and set in motion. I had expected your school to take care of any problems that arose. It's not normal that a boy like Helmut won't sing any more, from one day to the next. There's no reason, unless ... But whatever the reason, wouldn't it be your task, Dr. Wright, to solve the problem?"

"Certainly, all of us are here to solve the problem." The man who had to be the school psychologist, spoke for the first time, his voice as doleful as his eyes. "A problem with deep roots, you will agree. How a child deals with a new situation, new challenges and complications, depends on many things. There is a child's temperament, character, background, education. To put it into one word: it is a question of maturity. Maturity is the sum of a child's entire life." He paused. Kidcou's foster parents looked stricken. "As I indicated in my report, after thorough observation and testing, we have come to understand that Helmut has not yet reached the necessary maturity to enter our school and meet the challenges of this situation. He is, however, a very bright and gifted boy, and I am confident that in due time, he will be ready."

There was a pause. When will they talk about honor and tradition? Zelda wondered.

"Our offer stands," the headmaster picked up again. "It is only a question of time, and we will be honored to see Helmut take his place, a certainly brilliant place, within the ranks and the tradition of this school. I am convinced he will make us all proud of him."

He rose and everyone followed suit.

What a slimer, Zelda thought. Kidcou's been kicked out. That's what it all means.

On the way out, the headmaster approached Kidcou's foster mother.

"If you permit me to say a word as a parent myself, Madam. The healthiest place for young Helmut to be right now is in the bosom of his family."

She thanked him, but seemed a little flustered. He bowed deeply and opened the door for her and Kidcou's foster father.

Zelda wanted to follow them and hear what they were saying. She tried to push through the door, in vain. Her stomach turned. Something was forcing her to stay in place.

"Grasshopper!" she cried out angrily. "What are you doing?"

Everything was swaying. She noticed a window frame, a chauffeur at a steering wheel. She was riding in a limousine. The driver in his black cap and uniform was locked away behind a pane of glass. Kidcou's foster father, his back to the driver, was leaning on the large armrest of his seat, stroking his white mustache. Opposite him, his wife and Kidcou were riding side by side, both looking a bit lost in the ample seats.

Outside, many large trees were budding. Small fields between stone walls and hedges had gathered green fluff. Kidcou's foster parents looked the way they had before, in the headmaster's office. His foster mother was wearing the same hat. They had come to take Kidcou home.

"They kicked him out," Zelda addressed them. She wanted to get a conversation going. They clearly needed prompting. Kidcou was staring at his jacket buttons, his foster parents were looking out the window with the absent air of people who keep lots of thoughts to themselves.

"Why do they say I am too young?" Kidcou's voice broke the silence. "I'm eight, like the other boys." He didn't look up from his buttons.

His foster father cleared his throat. "It's a very demanding school. They mean that you need some more preparation."

"Where will I go now?"

"That's what we have to figure out. If it's for a semester or two, the best might be — I frankly don't know. Vienna?"

"Would you like to go back to Vienna?" His foster mother sounded encouraging.

Kidcou was silent. Zelda inspected him like a puzzle that needed to be solved. She shook her head at him. He sadly shook his head.

"You don't? But there's your beloved choir. You didn't want to leave, don't you remember?"

Zelda shook her head again.

"I don't want to go back to the choir."

"But don't you want to sing again?"

Silence. Zelda didn't know what to tell him. Kidcou's foster father stopped stroking his mustache. He shifted his legs with impatience.

"What's wrong, Helmut? Can't you tell us? One doesn't lose one's voice from one day to the next, just as one doesn't lose one's language. Or the use of one's legs. You still speak — so why do you refuse to sing?"

"I can't."

"But that's nonsense. Of course you can. Why do you keep saying that?"

Still Kidcou didn't raise his eyes. "Because ... I can't."

"The doctor assured us that there was nothing wrong with your voice. I just can't understand why you are doing this to — "

His wife's frown stopped him. He turned back to his window, to stroking his mustache, stroking back his words.

"Helmut, dear," Kidcou's foster mother put a protective arm around him, "we have asked you so many times, but you won't tell us. There is a reason, isn't there?"

The look Kidcou exchanged with her was probing, pleading. He faintly shook his head.

"There must be, my dear. There is always a reason. Nothing happens without one. If only you could trust yourself to us. Believe me, a gift like yours doesn't just disappear over night. Something must have happened to you. What is it, Helmut, that happened?"

Kidcou seemed to try as hard as he could and he also seemed to be at a loss. His foster father leaned forward in his seat.

"Tell us the truth, Helmut," he said. "We have always trusted you. Would you really want to let us down in such a way?"

Kidcou's effort to speak started to resemble his grimacing effort to sing. Then something broke in his face.

"I can't, I can't," he cried out. "I never want to go back there. Never. Never." He threw himself onto his foster mother's lap.

His foster mother patted his back with a thoughtful smile.

Her husband shook his head. "You were right," he said. "That darned school."

"Yeah," Zelda said.

After a while, Kidcou's foster mother sent her husband a look of warning. Then she declared, "You will never have to go back there. Do you hear me, Helmut? We won't send you back if you don't want to go."

Her husband lifted his hands as if to say, *And now what?*

"Maybe the headmaster was right," she continued. "Helmut should not be in school for a while. He should be in a family. With other children. Perhaps with some lessons. Someone who speaks English, certainly. I have had an idea." She had the air of a fine, silver-grey hunting dog as she waited for her husband to pick up the scent.

He frowned and pursed his lips. "Give me a clue," he said.

"His uncle twice-removed. The Italian line." She smiled. "Well?"

"Uncle Carlo!" Zelda shouted. "Italy! Let's go, let's go!" She stopped herself in time to hear Kidcou's foster mother say, "Carlo Contini."

"I see." Her husband nodded, impressed.

"Come on, Kidcou," Zelda prompted. "Uncle Carlo! Hurry up now."

Kidcou lifted his face. His eyes were brimming with the faintest hint of hope.

PART III

TAKE ME TO ITALY

CHAPTER 13

If this was Italy, it was hot. As hot as California where Zelda came from. The difference was that she wasn't thirsty. She scanned the open end of the station hall. Not a trace of a canal or an island. She might as well be in some run-down part of Los Angeles.

She followed Kidcou out of the train into a blur of dark heads and tanned faces. She recognized Uncle Carlo by his glasses with the snail-horn threads. He looked exactly the way she had expected him to look. Everything about him was round, up to his bald head with its crown of curly white fluff above the ears. His quiet smile stood out among the shouts and laughter washing over Kidcou. Part of the group on the platform spilled into the train to retrieve Kidcou's luggage, another arrived with a big bottle of water that was passed first to him. A giggly teenager produced a huge, scarlet slice of watermelon from a basket. A young man with the beginning of a mustache cut into the slice and handed Kidcou a piece on the tip of his knife.

Arriving in Italy was a feast celebrated right on the station platform. And the party kept growing. People with and without luggage stopped to join in. Most of them looked like they were from the same dark-haired, tanned family. The Italian language seemed to consist of the same exclamations, some familiar, others not. Zelda's ear caught uncountable "*ecco*!"s, "*ciao!*"s, and "*benvenuto!*"s. The word "*Elmuto*" was repeated so many times that she figured Elmuto was Helmut in Italian.

Elmuto took a shy, but visible pleasure in the welcome. This new family, "the Italian line," received him like a prince. He was hugged and his hair was touched by almost everyone. It was true, there wasn't another wheat-head to be spotted in the whole station.

Zelda wanted to join in and be welcomed, too. It was an odd sensation to be there among them, filling whatever free space opened up in the circle. She could feel her T-shirt glued to her back. She could smell dust, sweat, the metallic odor of the train, the sun-warmed straw from the hat of an ample, grey-haired woman next to her.

"Hello," she ventured to the straw hat that was swooping down to Kidcou at that moment. "Hi," she waved at Uncle Carlo, hopping up and down for emphasis. Her presence was not noticed even though she was there in a way she hadn't been before, when she was observing from a distance. It was exciting, like sitting in a movie theater and suddenly entering the action on-screen. It was confusing, too. She hadn't realized at first that the Grasshopper was present, too. Discreetly at a distance, the cello case at her side, she was standing among the other travelers at the station. A peculiar look from Uncle Carlo in the Grasshopper's direction had made Zelda turn her head.

For a second, she had the distinct impression that the two of them were plotting something. What were they up to? How could the Grasshopper be seen by Uncle Carlo when she herself was invisible? She left the circle and joined the Grasshopper for an explanation.

"We have arrived," the Grasshopper said, a glint of complicity in her big, slanted eyes. She continued to smile in the direction of Uncle Carlo, then turned to Zelda. "Welcome to Italy."

Zelda stared at her. "But you are wearing his glasses! And he is wearing them, too!" The moment she said it, the glasses disappeared from the Grasshopper's face.

The next thing she knew she was gliding along a canal in a boat. The boat was all black. There was no rower, but the Grasshopper was there.

Zelda's stomach turned. The vertigo almost threw her overboard. The Grasshopper's eyes without glasses came very close. Her glance seemed to study Zelda and at the same time steady her. She felt a cool, grass-like touch over her forehead.

"Where am I? Am I dead?"

"You got scared, Zzzeldina. You are right here with me, in Venice, in Italy. You must have had a *déjà vu*."

"A daysha what?" She couldn't be dead if she had to figure out words.

"It means 'something one has already seen.' For instance, when one arrives in a place one has never been and yet, mysteriously, feels one knows. How can one know a place one doesn't know? It can be quite disorienting. Dizzzying even."

The vibrating words seemed to make sense. But whenever the Grasshopper explained something, some new mystery was added to it. Zelda squinted at her.

"How would you know that I know this place?"

"How do I know? Let me reply by asking you, Have you ever

noticed that most people, when they grow up, seem to know less and less?"

"You bet."

"Have you also noticed that very young people, children, ask questions because they want to know everything? But as they grow up, they begin to ask questions because they want to doubt everything?"

Zelda squinted a bit harder.

"They stop seeing what is in front of their eyes and, instead, look for what might be hidden behind it. Are you following me?"

"Don't say you are talking about me," Zelda protested. "You know I'm eight. Eight. Not a day older."

"I am glad we both know it, Zzzelda. We could not have traveled together if it were otherwise."

"You said you were wearing Uncle Carlo's glasses, but I saw that he was wearing them, too."

"Time leaps like grasshoppers leap, forwards and backwards, do you remember? And there are moments when past and present seem to leap across each other, giving us the impression that they are happening at the same time."

Zelda tried to get used to the new look of the Grasshopper's face. Her eyes seemed even larger without the glasses. "Can you see without them?"

The Grasshopper chuckled. "I could see you were scared by something you recognized."

Zelda had the uncanny feeling that the Grasshopper knew more than she let on. That there was something she wanted Zelda to recognize.

The Grasshopper's big eyes were watching Zelda attentively.

Now her hand went into her coat pocket and produced something that she slowly lifted into view. She held it up exactly where their gaze met.

It was a honey-colored glass pebble.

Zelda suddenly felt heat all over her. How could the Grasshopper know? Had she been spying on her, just as Zelda had spied on Kidcou and his marzipan breads? How could she know about Zelda's good luck charms when she was in the cage under the juniper hedge? Had she only pretended to be a prisoner and fooled everyone? Here she was staring at Zelda with her bug eyes, reading her mind, stealing her secrets. How dare she?

Something was pressing into Zelda's palm, inside her fist.

"It is no secret, Zzzelda. Old pieces of glass make you see but they also protect you from seeing too far, too fast. Some people use their colors to leave a place where they feel imprisoned. What is not secret cannot be stolen."

Whatever was inside Zelda's fist was sending out a strange coolness. Glass. How had it got into her hand? For a moment she wondered how the special pieces of glass had ever managed to get into the dusty alleys of her neighborhood.

"Remember what you know. There are allies: trees are allies, grasshoppers are allies, and so is the wind that carries messages between us."

Zelda unballed her fist and there indeed was the glass pebble, shaped like a smooth, flat cloud. It was a color she had never come across in her roaming. Lifted against the light it had a golden glow and yet, she could see the blue of the sky through it. Tiny air bubbles were caught in the glass, making it look like frozen honey lemonade.

"Old pieces of glass are friendzzz," the Grasshopper repeated, buzzing like the string of her cello. "People who know them can travel through them. But sometimes they can find it hard to come back. This old glass will protect you."

"What if I don't want to come back?" Zelda asked. "I think I like it here."

She held the glass pebble in front of one eye and peeked about, careful of what she might discover. They were following a narrow canal between old houses. The walls were peeling in blots and blisters, reminding her of the modern painting her art teacher kept in his office. He insisted the blotches meant nothing, but Zelda could see faces and twisted figures hidden in the paint, and she always spotted the red dog from hell in the lower left corner.

Soon she would discover what these walls were hiding. If she looked at them through the glass pebble, the honey-golden filter brought out patches of browns and pinks and greens that were finely lined and dotted with black. Seen with her naked eye the same walls seemed coated with a rash of moldy, poisonous grey.

Her father's warning never to stay too long in wet socks and shoes, flashed through her mind. These houses were standing in the wet up to their knees. They had to be dangerously sick.

Were the people living inside them in danger? There were rooms behind these walls. She could hear voices, a radio blaring. High up, above the canal, between battered window-shutters, lines of sheets and clothes crisscrossed, stiff from the heat. If they dropped, would anyone jump in to fish them out? The water didn't look exactly inviting. It had a pungent smell.

Peels of oranges, plastic bags and bottles, a rubber boot, lazily drifted by.

"It's hot. And I can smell things," Zelda said. "But nobody sees me. I am not here. Where am I, then?"

"This is the place you asked me to take you to."

"Are you sure? My Dad said Venice was the most beautiful place in the world or something."

"You will be able to see for yourself, now that you are here."

"But I'm not here. How am I supposed to — ?" Zelda forgot her argument.

The boat had turned a corner into a much larger canal that was filled with boats of all sizes. There were motorboats, barges, ferryboats. But most of the boats were black boats with long, narrow bodies and a high stem in front that looked like the neck of a bird, a heron or swan. Many of them were empty, tied up to poles in front of houses. Others were gliding along, pushed by rowers standing upright at the stern with a single oar. The boat she was riding in with the Grasshopper suddenly didn't seem uncanny anymore. Not even special. It looked exactly like all the other boats on the canal.

"*Gondolas,*" the Grasshopper explained. "The people of Venice have used them for many hundreds of years to move through their city."

Zelda had to squint hard to stop her words from tumbling out. Kidcou had been right. Every boat — except hers — had a rower and all the rowers were men.

"Rowing the gondolas is the profession of the *gondolieri,*" the Grasshopper continued.

Rowing these boats, a profession? They were almost all dressed in black, with black, broad-rimmed hats. Some were wearing white T-shirts. They were talking to the people they were carrying, turning this way and that, pointing to buildings close by and in the distance, shouting and greeting one another. One was leaning on his oar singing and the couple in the boat clapped and laughed.

How come she hadn't known what Kidcou knew? Zelda fought back a wave of envy. There was one thing that nobody knew. One of the rowers wasn't a man. Nobody knew that the Rower, her Rower, had called upon Zelda, guided her through the alleys, and now had guided her to her city, the city of the canals.

It was a message. She was going to find a treasure here. But it might be dangerous.

She carefully watched the other rowers. What traffic on this canal! It was like the main street of a city. The buildings the rowers pointed to were pale pink, and burnt browns and yellows, like the houses in the narrow, shabby canal, but here they kept their colors even when she didn't look through the glass. They were big as palaces, with columns and balconies. Some looked like castles from a fairytale book, with towers and high, pointed stained-glass windows in forbidding walls. The strangest of all were decorated with stone statues, some of them looking down stark naked from the rooftops. This must be what her father meant when he called Venice beautiful.

The poles that held the boats in place were painted in stripes like candy canes, only much prettier, white and pink, pastel-blue and yellow, each one crowned by a wooden ball in one of these colors.

Behind them, steps rose from the water and ended at heavy doors that were all closed. Where did these steps come from?

Where did they lead? Secrets were being kept at each end, she felt. Old secrets. The water was lapping over them, and the stone was majestic and bent like old kings who cannot die.

"I want to be here," she said. "Really here."

"I understand." The Grasshopper slightly bowed. "You are certainly on your way. However, remember that our last leap, although we reached our destination, has landed us still in the past. You observed your little friend's arrival. He will once again be your guide. Getting closer to the present, you may indeed come to feel more present."

Zelda kicked the boat with her heel.

"Why do you always tell me things that you aren't really telling?"

"I have to admit grasshoppers have a quizzzical way with words." There was the familiar chuckle of dry leaves. "Nonetheless, you can trust that we always tell the truth. Am I wrong in my understanding that we understand each other most of the time?"

"Grasshopper," Zelda pleaded. She was carefully choosing her words. "You promised to take me. You gave me the glass pebble. You don't have to worry about me now. I'm fed up — I mean, I don't need a guide. I don't want to depend on Kidcou. I've got things to do. I don't want to follow him around any more."

"Certainly. Once we are back in the present, or, in other words, once we have leapt forward from here to the time we choose to call the present, you will be able to follow nobody, or whomever you must."

Zelda squinted hard. "How come this boat goes all by itself?" She refused to use the word *gondola*. "How come this boat doesn't have a rower?"

"A rower." The Grasshopper cocked her smile. "Let's see. Not being quite here and yet, getting closer, could be the answer. Traveling in the past, we do not feel the usual weight of things. Certain thoughts alone can move us along invisibly, like a sail catching wind, do you seizzze my meaning?"

Zelda felt she had been moving like this all her life, every afternoon when she went roaming in the dusty alleys of her neighborhood. The Rower had shown her the place and how to go about it. Venice, Italy. Now she was here, if not quite there, but here enough to discover her treasure. She balled the glass pebble up in her fist again and looked straight at her companion.

"So where's the glass island?"

CHAPTER 14

This wasn't an island, it was a room with books from floor to ceiling. Could the Grasshopper leap through a bookshelf? For a second, Zelda had the impression of a sand-colored travel coat swishing through a crack between two books.

The room resembled her school science lab, with glass containers, tables, instruments, a human and several animal skeletons. She heard voices and slipped behind a pair of drawn curtains. Through a slit in the curtains, she saw Uncle Carlo's bald, round head with its crown of white fluff, rising from behind a battery of test tubes and a Bunsen burner. It was reassuring to see him wearing his glasses with the little threads that stuck up at his temples like antennae.

"Time for dinner, my friend. Any further research will have to wait until tomorrow, I am afraid." He rolled every "r" as if there were three of them instead of just one. If the Grasshopper's speech was a sort of buzzing, Uncle Carlo's was something like a purr and a rattle, a purrattle. Zelda scanned the room. This must be the house Kidcou had told her about, the house with the rubber boots at the foot of the stairs.

The curtains were heavy green velvet that touched the floor, with plenty of room to stand behind them at the window. The window went from the floor almost up to the ceiling. Through a cast-iron balustrade, she saw the water below. Another canal, a small, narrow one.

She peeked through the curtains when she heard Kidcou say, "I am not hungry." His voice came from behind a big stack of books on a table. The Grasshopper didn't seem to be in the room, unless she was indeed hiding somewhere in the bookshelves. Zelda needed to inspect those shelves. Should she risk it?

She stepped out from behind the curtains and slowly tiptoed through the room. Not a single creak of the large, dark floorboards to give her away. She wanted to examine the shelves with her hands, but it was once again her eyes that did the examining. Her eyes were busily fingering the books when suddenly a bell rang above her head. She jumped.

A little brass bell was attached to a string near the ceiling, and someone in another room must have tugged at it.

"What did I tell you?" Uncle Carlo said calmly. "Dinner time." He couldn't have noticed her jump.

"Not hungry, really, Uncle Carlo, not at all, at all."

Zelda went to look behind the book stack where Kidcou's voice came from. He was half-lying on the table. His head was resting on his forearms. In front of him, on top of a thick old volume, the grasshopper was sitting in its familiar cage.

"Holy goat," Zelda said under her breath. "Grasshopper! How did you —?" It suddenly struck her that this, again, was the past. How could she tell if the grasshopper was her Grasshopper? This critter from the past didn't even know her yet.

"You like this grasshopper, don't you?"

Now they were all standing at the table: Uncle Carlo, Kidcou and she.

"He must be lonely," Kidcou said. There was a pause.

137

"He?" Uncle Carlo raised his eyebrows. Zelda wanted to nudge him. Just what she would have said. "Lonely, yes, I think you are quite right about that." The "r"s were purrattling like little balls of fur.

"And bored," Kidcou added, pensive. "You always work, Uncle Carlo, and now you even have to work with me and give me lessons. So he has nobody to talk to all day."

"You are quite right about that, too. But I want you to know that I, too, learn quite a lot in our work together. I noticed that lately you have been spending time with this little specimen. Did you notice that ... he ... looks somewhat less lonely already?"

Kidcou nodded, his expression unchanged. The grasshopper produced a delicate whirr. Kidcou looked up at his uncle with an unspoken question.

"Isn't that interesting? Already addressing you? Well, there is nothing better than two lonely creatures keeping each other company. Let's go eat. And if you have eaten well, you can spend some more time with your new friend."

Kidcou shrugged as if to say there wasn't much hope for that. His face shut down as he rose from the table. Uncle Carlo patted him on the shoulder on the way out.

Zelda decided to follow them. She had some catching up to do. If Kidcou had made friends with the grasshopper "lately," this was another big leap. It was a nuisance that she never knew how much time had passed and what she had missed. She always forgot to ask.

After passing through a long, dark corridor, it suddenly struck her that she was indeed following them. Nothing was holding her back. She had walked up to the bookshelves without even noticing, and now she was walking along behind Kidcou and Uncle Carlo. What had happened? Could she now come and go as she pleased?

At this moment, the three of them entered a room where the tanned, dark-haired group from the train station was gathered. She could tell in an instant that nobody noticed her. Uncle Carlo's family sat at a massive dining table loaded with plates, glasses, carafes of water and bottles of wine. Zelda wasn't hungry.

It struck her that apart from that massive table and an old wooden sideboard, there was no furniture in the room. A mirror in a gold frame reflected the early evening light from the window. It was another door-like window, only here it was wide open and a dusty-yellow curtain framed it. The big, sparse room seemed strangely filled, Zelda couldn't tell whether with the voices, laughter, or the light pouring in.

Other voices rang out, perhaps from across the canal. There was chatter, music, the clatter of dishes, then, rising above the other sounds, the shrill call of birds. It was a sound Zelda had never heard before.

She went to the window and felt the hot, humid air brushing up against her. The birds were chasing by right under her nose, grey birds with silver stomachs and sickle-shaped wings. They rose and dipped down to the water in daredevil curves, almost touching the walls and windows along the narrow canal. Their shrieks seemed to raise the pitch and speed of the talking and joking at the table.

Kidcou had taken a place next to Uncle Carlo at the head of the table, near the mirror. They were ten, Zelda counted. The chair at the far end of the table was unoccupied, even though a plate and glass had been set for someone. Zelda took it. She could always move if another family member — or would it be Ms. Grasshopper? — should turn up. For the time being, it was a pleasant jolt to be seated among that big, noisy group as though she, too, belonged.

A carafe with water was passed around and, to Zelda's surprise, approached her glass. A little girl with blackberry eyes huffed and puffed with the effort not to spill. Zelda wasn't thirsty, which was odd, but the water splashing from the crystal carafe into her glass made her wish to grab the glass and down it. The girl did spill the water and there was a gleeful "humph" from the exact copy of that little girl seated right next to her.

Across the table, the teenager, whom Zelda recognized from the station, giggled behind her hand. The ample woman who had been wearing a straw hat said something encouraging and the little girl stopped pouting while her carbon copy stopped gloating.

"Look at that," escaped Zelda. Nobody looked. She bent over the table to study the girls.

"You are two eggs from the same basket," she addressed them. She liked her wise tone of voice. "No, you are two black-berries from the same tree — hum, bush. No, in fact you are two shoes from the same pair." That fit. Like shoes sporting a buckle on opposite sides, one girl wore a little bush of black hair tied up with a rubber band on the right side, the other on the left side of her head.

Each had a shaving brush growing from her head. Some-one must have marked them to avoid confusion. Was it their mother, the ample woman without the straw hat, who couldn't tell them apart? Or was it meant for the father, the thin man with the tired face who was leaning back comfortably in an undershirt, his one hand nursing a cigarette, the other caressing the hairless head of a baby in a highchair?

When you had no language and no introductions you had to go by your own clues to figure out who was who, like a detective. The baby was placed between the thin man and the large woman, which made them the parents. All the youngsters at the table had the same blackberry eyes and had to be their kids. The only other grown man, Uncle Carlo, looked too old for the part of the father and was, of course, the uncle. What a thrill it would be, Zelda thought, to be part of a pair of identical twins. They would change the side of their shaving brush as often as they liked to trick everyone, especially their parents who would never know whom to blame.

The teenager had fetched a gigantic plate of spaghetti with meatball sauce from the kitchen. The excitement rose as the plate moved down the table and everyone started eating. Everyone except Kidcou. He was dreaming out the window, looking whiter than ever, at least in contrast to his new family. He also looked thinner. His baby cheeks had all but disappeared. How much time had gone by since his arrival at the station?

"Hey!" Zelda announced across the table. "He isn't eating."

The motion of forks whirling around in pasta, heads bending toward plates, stopped sharply. Zelda was going to duck under the table. Then she noticed it wasn't her announcement that had made everyone stop and stare at Kidcou. It was a large gesture from the mother.

Her stout, brown arm had shot out toward Kidcou's untouched plate in a gesture of pain and accusation. Soon, a torrent of outraged words followed, among them the familiar "*ecco*" and many plaintive "*Elmuto*"'s directed at Kidcou as much as at Uncle Carlo. Something seemed to be Uncle Carlo's fault. A word sounding like "munndja" was repeated over and over.

Finally, it was picked up by everyone in chorus. Shouting "*Munndja! Munndja!*" seemed to be a game, and perhaps the only way of drowning out the mother's wailing. Kidcou's other table neighbor, a youth with dark fluff on his upper lip, who had to be the oldest son, laughingly closed Kidcou's fist around the fork and swung it toward his plate in the rhythm of the chorus. Zelda guessed the word meant, "eat!"

An old woman in black who had to be the grandmother, reached over and pushed Kidcou's plate closer to him with her knuckles, revealing her missing front teeth as she crowed, "*Buono, buono!*"

The only adult who hadn't stopped eating was the thin man, the father, who had already almost finished off his plate.

Kidcou looked at Uncle Carlo for help. He didn't seem embarrassed, rather as if this were a tiresome routine he had to go through. Zelda wondered why he didn't talk. What the heck was wrong with him that he felt "lonely," as Uncle Carlo had called it, in the middle of this big, boisterous family?

"No 'ungry?" the youth tried to assist him, picking up an olive from a bowl and handing it to Kidcou on the tip of his knife. He had been cutting the melon at the station, Zelda realized. Kidcou shook his head. "No 'ungry," the youth repeated for the mother, while Uncle Carlo lifted his hands and shoulders in innocence. The mother began wailing again.

Zelda felt it was the right moment to join in and exercise her Italian. "No 'ungry? Ecco, eccoco. No 'ungry! *Madonna!* Elmuto crazuto sheeputo! *Ciao, ciao Madonna! Ah, basta spaghetti!* Yak!"

The baby started bawling. Perhaps Zelda's Italian was too much for it. That couldn't stop her. She rose onto her chair shouting and directing the debate as though it was the famous boys' choir, shaking an invisible handkerchief at anyone not talking. Mostly Kidcou, of course. He was staring out the window. He was with the birds.

Nobody seemed to notice (although Zelda gave ample notice with her invisible handkerchief) that one of the little girls had sneaked around the table, equipped with her fork. Her shaving brush suddenly appeared behind Kidcou's chair, from where she impaled a particularly promising meatball on his plate.

"Wello bello!" Zelda directed her back to her seat with her bounty which was enthusiastically shared by her twin. Kidcou sent a hint of a smile over to them. The other little girl promptly set out with her fork.

"Eat a bit, try," Uncle Carlo said, tapping Kidcou's hand. "Remember your reward." He winked as Kidcou stuck a fork into his plate, caught hold of a noodle and tediously slurped it up.

"*Ecco!*" came a big sigh from the mother, repeated by everyone else including Zelda.

The youth with the fluff of a mustache grinned at Kidcou and demonstrated the art of winding the slippery food around his knife-tip. Zelda could tell Kidcou didn't really try. He didn't care. He used his "trying" as a way of keeping occupied with the food that didn't end up in his mouth, and he succeeded well enough to distract the attention of the mother, guardian of the plates. The teenager, the older sister who giggled the whole time, went to putter in the kitchen while everyone else returned to their meal.

"Fools," Zelda lectured them. "He's a hopeless case. And he knows it." She shut up because Kidcou seemed to look right at her for a moment. Then, she remembered his smug spaghetti performance for her and her parents at the Italian restaurant. A lot must have happened between then and then, she pondered. He certainly had not arrived in America with any lack of appetite.

CHAPTER 15

Zelda decided to check on the rubber boots Kidcou had mentioned. She found a staircase leading down to a large entrance hall. The entire room stood under water. The bottom of the big wooden entrance door looked gnawed up by shark's teeth. The room smelled of wet stone and mildew. Rubber boots in all sizes and colors stood on a stone bench next to the stairs in one long file like soldiers at attention. She counted them out: Uncle Carlo, the thin father, the ample mother, the toothless grandmother, the youth with the beginning mustache, the giggly teenager, the twins, and Kidcou.

She saw the brown water marks lining the walls. It was a queasy feeling to imagine the water rising and rising, the ceiling moving in on you. There were, of course, the stairs to escape to the floor above. If it were up to her, she wouldn't mind a foot or so of water in the house. You could have your boat right there, ready to go. Like a car in a garage. You only needed to open the door to ride out.

She went to choose a pair of rubber boots to cross the room. Not that she minded getting her feet wet; invisible feet didn't seem to care one way or another. She wanted to do what everyone else in the house did. There were four yellow boots of the same size. They were much too small, but invisible feet didn't care about size either.

It made her laugh to see her feet in tennis shoes stuck in children's boots from the past that weren't real and yet were really moving along with her. They took every step she took. She must be making some kind of progress. She wasn't able to touch anything with her hands but she was in touch with a pair of boots. Perhaps "being in the present," as the Grasshopper had called it, had to begin with one's feet. And then, she thought, a lot of things could happen ...

She waded to a window next to the door to look at the canal. It was anything but a stately canal. The houses were leaning in as if they wanted to take a bath in the murky water, but they didn't have permission. Several black beams across the canal kept the upper floors from leaning too far. There were steps outside the shark-toothed door. They weren't exactly grand, Uncle Carlo's steps. But any steps leading into the depth of water had a mystery, she felt. Flanking them, two tired, blue-and-white-striped poles with white balls on top stood guard. She had expected a boat like the Grasshopper's to be tied up to them, but there was only an ordinary motorboat.

She went back upstairs to search for the Grasshopper's hideout.

"Could I take him to my bedroom tonight?" She heard Kidcou from behind his stacks of books. "Then he wouldn't be lonely at all."

She carefully approached the table, ducking behind the stacks, just in case. The grasshopper in the cage looked the same, whether in past or present tense.

This couldn't be said about Kidcou, however. During her exploration of the rubber boots he had had a haircut and changed his clothes. Without warning, she had made another leap in time.

"Quite right, my friend," Uncle Carlo purrattled. He had pulled a comfortable armchair to the table with the grasshopper's cage. "But remember that nighttime is the time when I open this little door and let our precious specimen out."

"Couldn't we let him out in my bedroom?"

"We might, we might indeed. But first we would have to make the creature acquainted with your room. To make sure it wouldn't get confused and lost."

"Quainted," Kidcou repeated. "How do I do that, make him a quainted?"

Zelda sputtered. Uncle Carlo for some reason kept his composure.

"Let's say you take it ... him for a little while tomorrow, during the day. You put the cage on your table, he likes to have an overview. The next day, you let him stay a bit longer. After a few days, you take him for a little promenade around your room. Some grasshoppers are not so different from us humans, you see. They can get disoriented. Just like you and me when we come to a new place, right?"

Uncle Carlo pulled a bag of tobacco from his jacket pocket and began stuffing a pipe. "Once you have carefully introduced him to the corners, nooks, and crannies, you show him the window. He has to be warned of the danger, you see. We don't want to lose your new companion because he loses his head and heads out of the window."

Kidcou had been threading stalks of fresh grass through the wire of the cage. "I would never, never leave the window open!"

Uncle Carlo nodded. "We couldn't easily replace him. In fact, we could perhaps never replace him."

"He is special, isn't he?"

"You bet he's special," Zelda cracked. "He's a she! But you'll never know — unless I'm willing to tell you." She almost regretted that she couldn't tell him right away.

Uncle Carlo put his pipe on a saucer on the table and went to pull a book from the shelves. He thumbed through it. "*Ecco.* If you want to know about grasshoppers, everything is in here, with fine illustrations. Short-horned, long-horned, crickets, locusts. You will read about all their particularities. How unthinkably far — from the perspective of a human being — they can leap and how some of them can travel across entire continents. This little specimen, however, has traveled farther than any one of its kind."

"And he chirps in English," Zelda added.

"Its nationality, so to speak, is French," Uncle Carlo continued. "You, too, are quite a traveler, as we know. You have been in France, in the countryside, haven't you? Who knows if your paths haven't already crossed? One of the many grasshoppers that you must have come across in the meadows might have been this very one."

Kidcou had forgotten about his stalks.

"I think our pass has crossed, Uncle Carlo," he declared.

He had got it almost right. Zelda looked at him with interest. So did Uncle Carlo.

"*Possibile.* Very possibly. After all, yours and mine have crossed well before you came to live with me and my sister's family. I know you don't remember. You were a very small boy when I first set eyes on you. That was in Paris, France, when your parents were still alive."

There was a silence. The woman and man in the picture suddenly seemed to be in the room, looking on.

"That was when you found the grasshopper?" Kidcou finally said. Zelda guessed he was trying not to talk about his parents. He had never mentioned them to her.

Uncle Carlo lit his pipe. "Back then," he paused to suck in air, "I found you, which was good luck," another few sucks, "for both of us, wasn't it? We wouldn't be here together if it weren't for an old family friendship between your parents and me.

"Your father had some Italian blood, as you may know. He was a *cugino*, a distant cousin of mine. Your mother, of course, was *tedesca*, German. They were a lively couple, your parents, always up to something, hungry for the world. They would come over in a friend's airplane for a night, for some grand performance at the opera, at *La Scala* in Milan, or here at our beautiful Venice opera house, *La Fenice,* which you know already. Afterwards we would talk late into the night about music. They would fly back the next morning at dawn."

"And fall down," Zelda humphed. "Leaving their kid in the dump."

Kidcou was busy again with his stalks.

"I remember the time when your parents spent a whole season in Paris and I came over for a conference. That's when I met you and I could tell, music for you was already like the air you were breathing. Your mother had given you a child's xylophone, and she would sing you the old song about the toadstool, the 'little man standing in the forest on a single leg, wrapped in a purple cloak' — *come si chiama*, what's it called again?"

"*'Ein Männlein steht im Walde'*..." Kidcou was by now half-lying on the table, not looking at his uncle.

"*Ecco.* She sang that song to you when I was there, and you banged along on your xylophone and promptly hit the right keys! Nobody had taught you. You had the ear of a musician, and you were no more than two years old. Can you believe it?" He tickled Kidcou's ear and Kidcou crinkled his nose. "Your father couldn't get you to the piano fast enough after that. You can imagine. But your mother disagreed. Let him find his own way, she would say. She had sewn you a purple cape with white dots, and when she came to the question in the song, 'Say, who could the little man be?,' you would bang on your xylophone and shout, 'Me! Me!'"

Kidcou now hung on his uncle's words as though unsure how to take it in.

"Then she would laugh and say, 'That's right, my little mush-room, but you are not alone!' And she would scoop you up," he swerved his arms out in Kidcou's direction, "and hug you tight."

He sat back and relit his pipe. "You were a happy child. *Si si*, that's what you were, even if you may not remember. When they were gone, you would not touch the piano again. But you picked up singing."

The silence had become thick and hot. Two red dots had appeared on Kidcou's cheeks. Uncle Carlo calmly went on puffing.

"I don't ... remember," Kidcou said in a voice that betrayed his effort.

"You mean, you don't remember them?"

Kidcou's bangs were too short to fall into his eyes. Zelda saw in them what she suddenly, now felt herself. It was impossible not to remember that woman in the photo. Her smile. Her eyes. How could he have forgotten? Not to remember her meant having lost her twice.

"*Senti*, listen well, my boy," Uncle Carlo said after a moment. "It is not your fault that you cannot remember. It is the way memory works. Few people remember anything from their lives before the age of three or four. That is a fact, *e un fatto*. A scientific fact. But later, too, when the brain is fully developed, it can happen that we do not remember. Even when we are adults. The brain is a storage house where things can get placed into a back room, so to speak. Painful things especially can come to be stored away from memory. This way we protect ourselves from knowing what we do not want to know. Much the way we draw a curtain over something we cannot bear to see."

Kidcou was sliding forward on the table, inching toward his uncle. He didn't betray whether he understood the purrattle. Zelda tried to remember what she remembered. Nothing. The only thing she remembered was her decision to be eight and never a day older. Before that, a blank. So if there was a storehouse and a curtain, as Uncle Carlo claimed, there might be slits to peep through. Slits of memory.

But then what? He was talking about some secret, something she would have to figure out. Uncle Carlo seemed to be handing her clues. Could he possibly know that she was there?

"The brain is a marvelously complicated thing," Uncle Carlo picked up again. Through the puff of smoke his narrowed eyes gave him the air of a large, white fox. "It is constantly fed and filled with information from our senses. What we see, hear, smell, taste, and feel is all registered in the big storehouse. You may have noticed that you can sometimes smell something and know right away: Ah! This reminds me, reminds me ... You may not be able to name it, but you know that you know that smell. Isn't that so?"

Kidcou and Zelda nodded.

"The same of course is true with a taste, the tone of a voice, a particular color, a face. Some people call it *déjà vu*: something one has already — ?" He pointed his pipe at Kidcou.

"Seen!" Kidcou said, surprised.

"*Ecco*! There you are. A French word that all of a sudden showed up again from long ago. And you didn't even know it was there, in your memory, right?" He gave Kidcou's forehead a light tap with his pipe.

"I know it, too!" Zelda exclaimed. She felt certain that Uncle Carlo was trying to tell to her something. "I know this daysha voo. Maybe I, too, have been in France ... "

"I see you are following me. So, let's come to a conclusion. You can know many things in this mysterious way. It is a form of remembering, a little bit like dreaming. It tells you that your experience is not entirely lost."

A mystery, a dream, a memory, a loss. Zelda concentrated hard to remember the clues. Taken altogether, she sensed the hidden meaning in his words. Uncle Carlo was comforting Kidcou for something lost in the past, but not just in the past. Something was going to happen soon.

"Your parents, too, are not entirely lost, you see?" Uncle Carlo continued. "They are in many ways in your memory; they certainly are in your music, *e certo*, in your laughter, in your fondness for this little specimen in its cage."

Kidcou slid onto his uncle's knee, and a big arm came around to enfold him. He did not move, but an almost imperceptible trembling rippled through him like a seaquake.

There was no sound, just the ticking of a clock, and every now and then a gentle muttering from Uncle Carlo who was smoking his pipe and patting Kidcou's head. Zelda carefully put a finger into the white crown of Uncle Carlo's hair that looked like silk fluff. Did he notice? When he scratched his head she didn't jump.

A whirr from the cage made Kidcou lift his head to look at the grasshopper. The critter made a hop.

"I say, your friend seems to be trying to cheer you up," Uncle Carlo said.

Kidcou slid down from his uncle's knee and leaned over, his face next to the cage. He whispered something Zelda didn't catch.

"Talking to him, you may remember your French," Uncle Carlo nodded, emptying his pipe onto the saucer. "And who knows, you may learn to speak Italian. Which, I noticed, you already understand quite well. Even if you don't let everybody know you do."

"I can teach you," Zelda sprang up from behind Uncle Carlo's chair, relieved that there was no more talk about remembering parents. "*Ecco eccoco*," she declaimed, "*Madonna, va bene, ciao tombola*. Grasshoppero knowo Elmuto wello bello, I you tello."

Kidcou looked at his uncle from under his lashes.

"*Non posso*," he said.

It sounded distinctly Italian. Zelda's lesson had made an impact. So why did he look defeated again? Perhaps he was confessing that he had been 'playing possum' at the dinner table.

154

His uncle ruffled Kidcou's hair with a chuckle.

"It will come, it will come. Everything in its own sweet time."

"Stoppo nonposso or I'll get crosso," Zelda commanded and made a few skips toward the bookshelves. The Italian language seemed to make one skip. "Stoppo nonposso!" She got carried away and lost her rubber boots. She hardly heard Kidcou say good-night. But she heard the grasshopper who was chirping in perfect attunement with her skipping.

"Did you bring in these boots?" Uncle Carlo's voice made her spin around. She stared at the yellow rubber boots scattered in her passage.

"No," Kidcou said, nonplussed.

"Has Nina been in here? Or Tina? They know they are not supposed to enter the lab."

Zelda took a breath. Nina would point at Tina, and Tina would point at Nina. Their parents would shake their heads the way Uncle Carlo was doing while he accompanied Kidcou to the door.

"Good night, my lad," he said.

"I'll show him my room tomorrow," Kidcou replied.

Uncle Carlo went over to the grasshopper's cage, still shaking his head. Muttering something, he opened the gate. The grasshopper came out onto the table in hops, like a pet, wagging its antennae. Then, with a sudden gigantic leap, it went straight into one of the rubber boots. This was better than the circus. Zelda was going to clap when she noticed that Uncle Carlo took up the boot, suspicious, and inspected the room as though he was sure something was not as it was supposed to be.

Zelda grew nervous. He was talking to the boot, or rather,

155

to the grasshopper inside the boot, in a language that did not sound like Italian at all. And now he was holding and aiming the boot around the room like a divining rod. She shrunk back expecting an alarm to go off the very second it was pointed at her.

Instead of a siren, however, something came right at her at great speed. She saw it the second it was so close there was no escape. A projectile with huge eyes. The grasshopper went right through her. Air, motion, speed rushing through her, blew her over. Nothing had touched her, but she fell.

CHAPTER 16

Wind was moaning. A door banged shut. It was the door to Uncle Carlo's lab. Zelda found herself in the hallway. How had she got here? She heard Uncle Carlo shouting. Kidcou came running out screaming "Vittorio! Vittorio!" at the top of his lungs.

She slipped through the door just before it banged shut again. The room was strewn with papers. A plant was blown over, the soil spilled across the floorboards. She suddenly remembered, she had fallen, here, in this room. The grasshopper had leapt at her. Why? To get her out of the room so she wouldn't be detected? But Uncle Carlo already knew she was there. The thought made her dizzy. What were they plotting? She had been frightened. Had the Grasshopper sent her some kind of a warning?

A strong draft came from a window. The dark green curtains were drawn, and one half of the window was wide open. Uncle Carlo was leaning over the cast-iron balustrade, holding his head. He was gesturing toward the room, to Kidcou who came rushing back in, followed by a good part of the family. Vittorio, the youth with the little beard, was at the helm, the two carbon-copy girls in tow. Only the father, the baby, and the grandmother were missing. The draft blew the other half of the window open, the curtains billowed, and the door banged more violently than before.

Everyone was crowded into the window. There were hushed screams, "*O no!*" and "*Madonna!*" Zelda had to make an effort to squeeze through even though she didn't take up much room, being invisible. She followed everyone's stare out the window. Midway across the canal, on one of the beams that kept the houses from leaning into each other, sat the grasshopper, a little green speck against the blackened wood.

"*Non e possibile,*" The ample woman, who was Uncle Carlo's sister, gaped as if she were having a vision.

Vittorio pushed several "*maledizione!*" through his teeth, and the teenage girl crossed herself each time. Uncle Carlo explained something in a low, but agitated voice, repeating the word "*tempesta*" and shaking his fist at the sky.

Zelda understood. The storm was a pest. But she liked storms, especially this one. The rush of air, the noisy banging, had slapped her right back to her senses after her fall.

"The window blew open first thing when I opened the door this morning," Uncle Carlo explained to Kidcou. "The grasshopper must have been right there already. It likes the green curtains. If it jumps again and hits the water it will drown." He went on speaking Italian to his sister and her family, still keeping his voice low. A lot of waving and clasping of hands and pointing of fingers followed. Their voices soon reached a pitch that told her they didn't know what to do.

"Are you sure, *sure* he can't swim?" Kidcou interrupted anxiously.

"The spiracles! Its breathing holes! They fill with water very fast. With this choppy surface, we wouldn't even see its landing. How could we fish it — him — out in time?"

Uncle Carlo's face was red. Zelda looked down again and

saw that there was nothing to land on after a jump from the beam. Just water, a dark grey, boiling glue. The sky was grey, too, with low, racing clouds, threatening rain. Even without a leap, she thought, a gust of wind might carry the grasshopper away at any moment. She suddenly understood why the Grasshopper had come in a cage. In the shape of an insect, she was vulnerable. And perhaps her judgment was off.

"We have to get there. With the cage. Some way. With fresh leaves in the cage. There is a chance. She ... he may return. The way he normally does. Every morning." Uncle Carlo's purrattle was choppy like the canal. He seemed to have difficulty breathing. "*Dio mio.* If we could find a way. To get to him. *Non e certo. Ah, la tempesta!*" He switched back and forth between Italian and English. "He's in an unknown environment. *E molto pericoloso.* How can we know. Whether he still recognizes water. For what it is. *Mortale!*"

Kidcou listened, aghast. Uncle Carlo looked quite out of sorts, his shirt buttoned the wrong way, his white fluff of hair flying into his eyes, mingling with the threads of his glasses.

"The cage is our only chance. But how to get to him?" Uncle Carlo turned to the canal again, wiping his forehead.

"Vittorio!" His mother shrieked as the young man flung a leg over the balustrade, ready to go.

Everyone froze and stared down. But the grasshopper hadn't stirred. A fierce argument erupted. Vittorio's mother would rather throw herself out of the window, Zelda read the gestures, than let him go out onto that beam. Who could be insane enough to imagine that this miserable piece of wood could carry the young man's weight?

"It won't do, won't do." Uncle Carlo leaned against the window frame, holding his chest. "Concetta?" he meekly proposed.

Concetta, who had not giggled in the longest time, drew in her mouth like a fish. She silently implored her mother who raised her pitch anew against her unreasonable brother. Nina and Tina were following the debate like a Ping-Pong match, their shaving brushes whisking from one side of the argument to the other. Zelda was wondering how her weightless body would do on the beam. She was ready to offer her services when Kidcou said, "I'll go."

"Elmuto!" The youth stared at him in disbelief, and so did the whole family who had got the message, even in English. Another debate followed, interrupted by Kidcou's determined and increasingly urgent, "I'll go. Please. I want to. Let me go."

Uncle Carlo gave Kidcou a long, probing look. Then he took a breath and recovered his usual collected self. He took command, gave quick orders, prepared Kidcou.

"*Alora*, Vittorio will go get the boat, just in case you lose your balance. Don't be scared, my boy. *Va bene*. The beam is strong enough to carry you. All that matters is that you get down on it without any bumps or shakes, and that you move very gently. No sudden jerks — you understand? Any shock could ruin it. Talk to it, I mean, him, once you are in position. Lull him into trusting you, and just slowly, steadily advance the cage. *Capisce?*"

Kidcou nodded, biting his lips.

Uncle Carlo picked a few leaves from the plant that was scattered over the floor, placed them in the cage, and fixed the open door with a grass stalk so it would not be blown shut by the wind before it was time. The teenager with a name like Confetti had run to fetch a piece of washing line which

Uncle Carlo tied to the top of the cage.

Finally, the cage was hung around Kidcou's neck and Uncle Carlo and his sister lifted him onto the window balustrade. The *tucker-tucker* of the motorboat could be heard around the corner. As soon as Vittorio had positioned the boat alongside the wall, close to the beam, Kidcou was lowered out the window by his arms.

He got almost low enough to sit. At a signal from Uncle Carlo, his sister let go of Kidcou's one hand in order to lower him further. But his free hand still wasn't able to reach around the unwieldy cage and get hold of the beam. He was hovering in place, uncomfortably arched backwards, pulled up by his uncle's supporting hand, afraid to let go.

"Lean back against the wall," Uncle Carlo advised. "The wall will steady you when I let go. Ready? *Ecco.*"

For a second, Kidcous arms rowed the air for balance. Zelda held her breath. Then he swung them forward and grabbed the beam without letting the cage hit the wood.

"*Eccellente*, my boy," Uncle Carlo said. "Now move forward, gently, dolce, dolce."

Kidcou began inching his way towards the center of the beam where the grasshopper was still in place. Both sitting, facing the same direction, they were an odd pair of creatures riding the beam: one tiny, one big; one with long, waving antennae, the other with a cage swaying around his neck like a huge, misshapen cow-bell. The cow-like creature was inching closer when a sudden shout from a window in the opposite house startled everything to a halt. The neighbors had caught sight of the big creature approaching their house through midair. One window was opened, then another. Anxious voices

162

flew back and forth while Uncle Carlo and his sister tried to explain and shush everyone up.

"Don't worry, Elmuto, just move on," Uncle Carlo assured Kidcou.

"I right 'ere," Vittorio shouted from the boat.

Kidcou set into motion again. He was trying hard not to look down at the angry water, Zelda saw. He was also trying not to look at the neighbors in their windows.

Every now and then he fought with the gale and the swaying cage. A hushed chorus of "Oh!"s and "Ah!"s and "*Dio Mio!*"s accompanied each of his hesitations. Kidcou's headway seemed to inspire the grasshopper into motion, too. Now they both moved in the same direction on the beam, looking like a circus procession on a tightrope.

"He won't stop!" Kidcou cried out in anguish. He had almost reached the midpoint of the canal.

"Remember to talk to him. *Parla*! Say anything," Uncle Carlo urged.

"I can't. I don't know how." Kidcou was pale and sweating. He tried to look back at his uncle for help but he could not turn his head without losing balance. Zelda saw enough of his face to know that he was exhausted.

"Don't stop, Kidcou," she called out. "Don't give up. Just sing to the hopper." She imagined shooting her idea like an arrow right into his head.

"That's right. Do it, my boy." Uncle Carlo, to Zelda's surprise, seemed to join in. "Remember."

Zelda showed him how, "Grasshopper, don't move away from me. Come let us stay in Italy!"

If only she could sing on key. It made her self-conscious to belt out a song in front of so many people, even if they couldn't hear her. Perhaps Kidcou, too, was self-conscious, although he had no reason. He sang perfectly on-key, had done it all his life, in front of whole rooms full of people. The boys' school flashed through her mind.

"You are not a duck!" she shouted. "The Grasshopper likes singing. She came to me because I was singing to her."

The grasshopper had stopped. Its antennae were scanning. It was listening. Zelda took a deep breath in order to sing louder. Then she noticed the high tone. It came though the wail and rattle of wind, wavered, broke off, was gone. Then it was back, steadying itself, cutting through the menacing air like a thin thread of light. There was a melody, torn this way and that. It came from the beam. Kidcou was singing.

The grasshopper turned around. Now the two creatures were facing each other across a small distance. Zelda almost fell into the canal. They both must have heard her.

Shreds of melody came wafting over her. It was a mournful melody, like the song of someone lost at sea. Uncle Carlo, his face red, was gripping his chest trying to breathe. His sister and the teenager were clutching each other's shoulders. Nina and Tina stood pressed against the balustrade, showing the tips of their tongues in the same corners of their mouths.

The grasshopper seemed to be drawn to the sound, step by step on its long, pointed legs, as the melody kept calling. Kidcou had stopped advancing. He slowly bent forward until the cage squarely rested on the beam. He seemed to have forgotten where he was and that there were people around. More people, Zelda noticed, crowded into the windows. Crossing themselves. Listening to the song that reached higher and higher, the closer the grasshopper got to the cage.

He's casting a spell, Zelda thought.

A shudder, a collective sigh of awe — the grasshopper had entered the cage. The sight dug a strange claw into Zelda's chest. She had told Kidcou what to do, and now the creature had turned its back on freedom and returned to its prison. For what? Had the Grasshopper given up, afraid to die in the storm? It was impossible to believe.

The Grasshopper's magic was much too powerful. Whatever she did, she did it on purpose. Purpose was the first thing she had asked Zelda about. Zelda suddenly saw it clearly: the Grasshopper had come back for Kidcou. On purpose. The claw dug deeper. Somehow it was Kidcou who had been saved. And Uncle Carlo, too, for whom Kidcou had gone out on the beam. They were all three in on this together.

And where was she?

She shook herself. This was Kidcou's past. Her purpose was to follow him until she was out of the past, not a moment longer. Then she would be free to look for her treasure. She had to remember. The Grasshopper had come to America to be freed … by her.

She squinted. Kidcou was still in the same position in mid-air, his legs wrapped around the beam, his head resting on the cage. His hand slowly pulled the grass stalk from the little door and closed it.

There were a few shouts and bravos, quickly hushed by Uncle Carlo whose face was still worried.

"*Va bene.* Well done, my boy. Now pull your head out, carefully, and extend the washing line. Secure the end around the beam.

Vittorio will be ready to receive the cage."

Kidcou slipped out of the carry-noose and, holding the cage between his thighs, set to work. He seemed to have forgotten about the height, his narrow support, the assault of the wind that could at any moment throw both him and the cage into the angry water.

Vittorio had steered the boat right below the beam, trying to hold his position.

"Ready," Uncle Carlo called.

Kidcou grabbed the washing line, inched the unwieldy cage to the edge of the beam, then threw his body forward at the exact moment he let the cage slip. It was perfect timing. The weight of his body, one arm clasped around the beam, counterbalanced the shock of the drop. He grimaced when the line cut into his hand. But he held on. Swaying, in little spurts, the cage sank toward the boat.

"*Ecco!*" Vittorio lifted his thumb. He grabbed the cage with a broad grin.

"Bravo! Bravo Elmuto!" The shouting and clapping drowned out the storm.

Kidcou dropped the washing line that went lashing overboard, into the water. He was lying on the beam like on the branch of a tree.

"Vanto leap?" Vittorio reached up with his arms. "I you catch."

"*Si!*" Kidcou shouted.

Uncle Carlo's sister grabbed his hand with alarm. The two girls hopped up and down, clapping, their shaving brushes bobbing. Vittorio signaled Kidcou to wait for the boat to reposition.

"*Attenzione!*" he called out.

Kidcou let his legs and body slide off. Shrieks from both sides of the canal accompanied his drop from the beam.

"*Avanti!*" Vittorio shouted into a brief lull of the wind and let go of the helm. Kidcou splashed into the water right next to the boat. To Zelda's surprise, he came up laughing. He'd done it on purpose. Vittorio fished him out like a trophy and turned the boat around. Now the chorus went: "Bravo Elmuto! Bravo Vittorio! Elmuto *campione!*"

Kidcou stood in the boat, dripping wet, shivering. Holding the cage with the grasshopper high up over his head, he beamed at Uncle Carlo until the boat had turned the corner.

CHAPTER 17

Seven tarts and cakes were arranged on the big dining room table. The largest one was a glistening chocolate cake with an inscription in creamy white letters, CONGRATULAZIONE ELMUTO. There were cookies on plates, berries in goblets, clouds of whipped cream in a silver bowl. Crystal decanters held what looked like liquor or brandy. There was the smell of fresh coffee. Above it all, on a throne of three big old books, sat the grasshopper's cage.

The room was packed with extra chairs. The entire family was gathered, the baby and the grandmother included, and they were joined by their neighbors. Zelda recognized some of the faces she had seen at the windows, across the canal. Uncle Carlo was talking, and everyone, standing or sitting, was listening. His arms went sweeping back and forth between the cage on the table, the window that was closed and wet with rain, and Kidcou who was standing at his uncle's side.

Zelda knew he was retelling the adventure of the grasshopper's escape and rescue, the story everyone knew and had seen with their own eyes. It reminded her of her father's fussing over his seedlings. This was Uncle Carlo's fussing over Kidcou. His listeners, however, didn't mind. They seemed riveted as if they hadn't been watching every move and shouting, "Oh!"and "Ah!" already.

It wasn't quite fair, this big deal, when Kidcou hadn't done it all by himself. Didn't she deserve a share? What if she hadn't convinced Kidcou to sing? It had been her idea. She knew about spells. But nobody knew about her. Why wasn't the Grasshopper, her Grasshopper, there to cock her head and smile approval?

Zelda spun her head around every now and then, but her eyes only caught the battery of cakes that topped Kidcou's forty-eight — or was it fifty-eight? — marzipan breads. Kidcou was a funny fellow. He either had nothing or he had more than anyone else. And now, he also had attention. Tons of it. He didn't seem to mind being hugged, patted, ruffled, squeezed and smooched by just about everyone in the room.

Vittorio had taken on the role of second hero of the day. His hair was slicked back, and he had donned a white shirt and black vest. He kept throwing in remarks in English, filling in parts of the story, and grinning around the room, the hair on his upper lip stretching and thinning like an accordion.

At the end, just as everyone got ready to clap and a few women crossed themselves, Uncle Carlo went into something that sounded like a toast. His hand on Kidcou's shoulder, he then addressed Kidcou in his furriest purrattle, "Courage — *coraggio* — is the same word in all the languages you speak, but we first met in France, and you saved the life of a grass-hopper from France. Therefore, I propose to give you a French name of honor. To celebrate an outstanding act of courage, your new name shall be *Courage, Kid Courage*."

Everyone rose for a standing ovation, repeating, "Kid Coo-raajh."

Zelda noticed that Nina and Tina made a blitz excursion under the table to the side where the cakes were waiting.

171

Each stuck a finger into the chocolate icing. She followed them and stuck a finger in, too. The girls' mother approached with a tray of plates and cutlery. She stopped. She stared at the three holes in the cake, two small ones and one big one. Nina and Tina exchanged a puzzled glance and dove back under the table.

Zelda licked her thumb in awe. It was a thick, dark, spongy featherbed of chocolate she was sinking into. What was happening to her? How could she taste anything? How could she touch anything? She squinted around. This was scary. What if all of a sudden she wasn't invisible anymore? What if everyone else noticed before she did? In that case, she would have a lot to explain. But how to explain that she knew Kidcou although he didn't know her because this was the past and they had only met in the future?

Someone else would have to explain it. All she cared about was sucking every bit of leftover chocolate from her thumb. This was too good to worry about anything. Let Uncle Carlo take care of it. Let the Grasshopper take care of it.

She had known right away at the train station that the two of them were plotting something. Maybe she even was part of their plot. Maybe because she was here, everything would turn out different. Kidcou's treasure wouldn't get lost, Uncle Carlo wouldn't die, and she would go on eating chocolate forever.

Everyone had approached the table to watch Kidcou drive a big knife through the chocolate cake's belly. While the grandmother helped him steer his piece onto his plate with the help of her knuckles, the baby, riding on its father's arm, pointed toward the action and crowed, "Kicoo! Kicoo!"

Nina and Tina, now above-table, nudged each other. They

picked it up in chorus, "Kidcou, Kidcou!" Their shaving brushes, sporting stiff pink ribbons for the occasion, stood guard as they pointed their fingers.

There was no way of resisting their excitement. Kidcou looked at his uncle, at Vittorio. He crinkled his nose at the twins, "Okay. Kidcou."

"Okay, okay, okay," they imitated him, hopping up and down until they got their cake. When everyone was served, the adults lifted their cups of espresso or glasses of liquor and made a toast to "Kidcou."

Zelda was impressed. Kidcou talked and ate, ate and talked. In Italian. Vittorio didn't leave his side, and the two of them prattled up a storm. She snatched a morsel from Kidcou's plate every now and then. He didn't pay attention. Everyone patted him, served him, asked him to show them the grass-hopper, to flex his muscles, and all the while he was eating and talking, talking and eating.

She went as far as stealing the bite of pie that he had just impaled on his fork and was holding in midair, ready to go into his mouth the moment he'd shut up. Being invisible was turning out to be fun. He looked at his empty fork, at his plate, at the floor. Then he grabbed what was left of his pie, crust and all, stuffed it into his cheeks and — Zelda had to give him credit for that — went on talking.

When the cakes were about finished off with Zelda's help, a neighbor intoned a song, inviting Kidcou to take over. Kidcou went pale. Zelda saw the old terror in his eyes.

"*Coraggio*, Kid Courage!" Uncle Carlo said.

Kidcou looked down. Zelda was afraid to hear him go "quaak quaak" again. In the moment of silence, while everyone was waiting for him, the storm threw a bucketful of rain against the window panes. Kidcou looked at his uncle.

"*Tutti*," Kidcou said, his voice hesitant. "Everyone."

Uncle Carlo nodded and joined in when Kidcou began, "*O sole mio...*" The whole group fell in immediately.

Zelda couldn't resist singing with a whole room full of people who could. They all knew this song that her father sang every time they went to an Italian restaurant. They all sang defiantly against the rain rattling against the window. As soon as the song ended, another one was proposed, and then another. Zelda noticed that Kidcou was able to pick up a new melody in an instant, after just one verse. How on earth did he do this?

As nobody could hear her, she sang at full throat, stomping and clapping along, growing happier by the moment. There was nothing like singing whatever came to her as loudly as she could, without being hushed up or eyed with a smirk. On the contrary, everyone looked pleased. Everyone sang louder and louder as well. She fit right in, like in a big, warm tub of water. Couldn't this be her family?, she thought in the middle of a refrain that made everyone bark like dogs, meow like cats, crow like cocks, and moo like cows. Why couldn't she have a family like this one?

All of a sudden, she was overcome by sadness. Here she was, all alone. True, she had wanted to get away with the Grasshopper, but where had that got her? She was not one bit closer to the glass island where her treasure was waiting for her. Wasn't she supposed to get a reward for setting the Grasshopper free?

Kidcou was lucky. His cheeks were red, his eyes were sending out sparks. His voice rose until it soared above the whole group like one of the birds of the city. Even the grasshopper in the cage sang, Zelda noticed with a renewed pang of loneliness. The chirping sounded eager, as though the critter had just now recovered from the shock of the storm.

"Grasshopper, Grasshopper, speak to me," she went into a singsong, sadly wagging her fingers like antennae. "Don't leave me alone in Italy ... "

"Your faithful servant, Zzzeldina."

She had to squint hard. The voice had come right out of the cage. Now the insect cocked its head and waved its antennae up just once and then down in a way that couldn't be mistaken. The Grasshopper was making a little bow to her from the cage.

CHAPTER 18

A moment later, the cage had opened into a huge square. It was so big and empty, it made Zelda seem like a speck, barely the size of a grasshopper. It was night, yet she could see. She was dizzy. She had to pinch herself to know she wasn't dreaming. Two sides of the square looked like they were made of gigantic paper doilies. As if someone had taken them from one of the cake plates at Kidcou's celebration and cut them into the shape of long rectangles with frilly little figures on top. The third side bulged with domes of thick, ruffled paper skirts. Had the Grasshopper leapt with her onto one of the cakes?

She looked again. Everything was wet and glistening. The whole square, in fact, was covered with water. She remembered, it had been raining. The frilly and bulging buildings were all growing right out of the water. Her heart beat faster. This was the city, the Sunken City. She listened to the silence and squinted in every direction. She was finally on her own. Or was she?

The only other creatures she could see on the square were perched on top of two high pillars. One was a flying monkey, or perhaps a lion with a monkey's tail. It was difficult to make out against the night sky.

The creature was turning its back to a human figure on the second pillar. This figure seemed to be holding a single tall oar and wore a hat like those of the many rowers of the canals. A he-rower on a boat that looked mysteriously capsized. Perhaps they were standing guard for the Empress of the Sunken City, a warning to anyone who might want to follow her uninvited.

Zelda slipped her hand into her Bermudas' pocket and felt for the glass pebble, just in case. In the background, beyond the gate, she saw the sea. Pockets of islands were sitting on it, filled with promises. One of them had to be made of glass. All she needed was a boat.

Where was the flurry of boats on the canals? Not a single one. There was nothing but water around. Noiseless water, lying in wait. Something was about to happen. Zelda squinted. The monkey-lion looked ready to fly to her defense should anything come at her.

"How do I get to the glass island?" she shouted up at the creature.

Nothing stirred. Perhaps the monkey-lion was cut out of paper after all, glued onto the rainy night.

"Monkey-lion, fly me there, ride me through the paper air," she tried her croaky singsong. How was she supposed to get around in the middle of the night all by herself?

"Grasshopper, if you don't talk to me, I don't want to stay in Italy," she continued her singsong. Trying to dispel her sense of eeriness, she skated across the sheet of water with her invisible feet, swishing around the footless lanterns. Way over, across from the pillars, were several round café tables. An empty beer can was lying on one of them. And that's where the Grasshopper was sitting, calmly, in her travel coat.

It gave Zelda a start to see her there. For a moment, she

was at a loss for words.

"Are you telling me you would rather go home, Zzzeldina?" The Grasshopper smiled her pointed smile.

"I didn't say that. Why do you always leave me alone?"

"I am always here." The Grasshopper waved her long, very long hand to the chair next to her. "Remember, all you need to do is call me up when you wish to converse, traverse or reverse."

"Not true!" Zelda refused to sit down. "You are never really here, and I am not really here, and I have nobody!"

"I see," the Grasshopper said, cocking her head as if to get a better look at Zelda. "What is it, do you think, that we could do about it?"

"Couldn't I also have an Uncle Carlo, and a Vito, and a whole big family like that?"

She saw the long dinner table in the room filled with light, filled with food and laughter, the many cakes, and the neighbors toasting and slapping their thighs and singing in loud voices. Then she saw her father in his apron, cleaning off the table that was aways loaded with her mother's files, while her mother was already back on the phone discussing the strategy of a case or planning a meeting. She saw herself doing the dishes with her father who would say his silly little sayings and tell jokes until she couldn't help laughing, and then she would feel bad because her mother would think they were having a really good time, she and her father, doing the dishes. There was something awfully wrong with that.

But everything seemed her mother's doing. She gave the directions like a general — although she didn't look the part with her tousled curls, especially when her eyes were a bit red from a glass of wine. Under her mother's command, they marched into the kitchen and out like wind-up toys, eagerly in step, but each one awkward and alone. Why did it have to be like that?

She looked at the Grasshopper who had an air of giving her all the time in the world to figure out her own mind.

"Kidcou gets everything and I get nothing," she wanted to say. But the words wouldn't come out. She averted her gaze. The paper doily facades around the square stared back at her, indifferent. She balled her fists in her pockets. If Kidcou didn't have a real mother and father, so what? She wasn't much better off. Only she didn't make a big deal out of it. She knew how to fend for herself and for what was fair, and she accepted the consequences. How come, then, she never got any applause for it? How come nobody showered her with marzipan breads?

She saw Kidcou trying mean-eyes, in vain, his eyes blueing. She heard him sobbing. She saw her mother's fond looks for him. Everyone found him cute. Uncle Carlo did. The Grasshopper too, she was sure of it. And she, what did she get for not being a crybaby? Nothing. She was invisible. It all came down to that.

The Grasshopper had bent forward on her chair as if she were keenly listening.

"Kidcou is like a girl and everybody goes gaga over him. And I am not like that. Nobody likes me." It was suddenly easy to let the words out of her mouth and not care one bit about their bitter taste. "My father pretends to like me because he tries to make peace that way and make up for my mother who can't make sense of me and who only likes Kidcou anyway. And you — " she swung back to the Grasshopper with a glare, "you too. You are no different really. Yeah, you took me to Italy, but that wasn't about me. Not *for* me. I bet you just pretended to be in danger on that beam. You did it on purpose. You and Uncle Carlo. To make Kidcou look like a hero with all that fuss over him when, in fact, he's a loser. I know he's going to lose his treasure. Why did you bring me here if it wasn't for him? To make me watch over him? To stop him? I won't! You only took me to Italy because you wanted to be back here, with Uncle Carlo and Kidcou!"

Something came over her that was unknown. Not the hot, familiar roar. What had been lying in wait on the square was quietly inching up her ankles, sneaking up her belly, pressing into her chest. She was pushing hard but she couldn't push it back down. It forced itself out of her mouth and nose and eyes in spurts of pain and there was nothing she could do about it. Her words, her weapons, her will — everything was gone. She didn't recognize herself. Helpless sounds kept spilling out. A wailing that didn't belong to her. She had to shut it up. Drown it. Throw herself down and get rid of it for good.

She couldn't tell what happened next. Water was rocking. Rocking up, kicking down. Up and down. She was riding in the Grasshopper's boat. She heard the cello. She listened for a long time before she peeked through the slits of her eyes.

The Grasshopper was sitting in the boat, holding the cello upright on her knee. She was striking the one string with her bow, then reaching around to pluck it. It sounded like drops of falling water. They were moving once again without an oar. The Grasshopper's big, bulging eyes were almost closed, reminding Zelda of paintings she had seen of angels playing mandolins. Something about the image reminded her of her loneliness.

"You always jump away from me," she said, peeping through the slits of her eyes. "Or you try to get me out of the way. You leapt at me on purpose, didn't you? To get me out of the lab, so you could be with Uncle Carlo. You are always plotting, the two of you."

The Grasshopper continued playing.

"You are right," the Grasshopper said. "It was all planned between my old friend Carlo and myself. You have a fine, perceptive mind, Zzzeldina. My leap out of the window on a stormy day, onto a beam too frail to carry anybody except your little friend. All this was plotted, as you put it, and prepared. However, nothing was known of the result. Would he be too frightened? Would he give up? Would he endanger himself and the grasshopper — me — with him? Who could have told? Sometimes it takes the greatest risk to find an answer that matters."

"But I did it, too! I told Kidcou to sing. Uncle Carlo didn't. *I* did. And he heard me. That's how he did it."

The Grasshopper cocked her head attentively. "With your help. Of course."

Zelda stared at her companion. She knew?

"Without you, if he had failed, imagine his despair. He might never have recovered his voice — or his spirit. Do you understand what I am saying? What was at stake? A boy lost, his spirit broken."

Zelda nodded. The image of Kidcou stuck in the position of a duck made it clear enough.

"You offered your help," the Grasshopper went on, "as only someone familiar with that kind of danger could offer it." She tipped the bow toward Zelda as if to illustrate an offering. "Do you realizzze? I am telling you something that is no secret and yet not everybody knows. The best help comes from a place of knowing."

Zelda wasn't sure what she was supposed to know or *realizzze*. But somehow the buzzing speech went down like a glass of warm milk with honey.

"There is another thing you know," the Grasshopper continued, "which is why you can't have what Kidcou has and what you told me you wish for — an Uncle Carlo and a whole big family like his. Remember this is the past. You are invited to enjoy it as long as it lasts." She waited for Zelda to follow her, then played a shrill tone that hurt as if the cello string was torn.

"Uncle Carlo!" Zelda sat up with a start. "He'll die. That's what you mean, don't you? I won't let it happen. That's why I am here, no? Grasshopper, let's do something about it."

"Even in a world where one is eight years old and not a day older," the Grasshopper said, "there is not much to be done when someone's time has come."

"But *not much* means there's still something ... "

"Something has already happened, you see. Had your little friend not found his courage and his voice — with your help — we would have to worry about him when the time comes to say good-bye to his uncle. How would he be able to bear it?" Her gaze enveloped Zelda. "Not without help. Not without allies, you understand?"

Zelda had a sense deep in her body that she herself might

not be able to bear it.

"That day of the storm, when your little friend's destiny was in question, you grew into an ally and reached into the past for a moment. As a consequence, you were able to taste the cake and hear me answer you from the cage. I am pleased to see you grow present in that way."

Again, Zelda felt warmth like milk and honey running through her. The Grasshopper knew. She knew everything Zelda had done. She, too, had been a hero of the day. Invisible, but the Grasshopper had seen her.

She took a deep breath, and looked around. They were at quite a distance from the city. The sky was grey. The sea looked sullen like a raincoat. But there were the pockets of islands sitting on it.

"You said when I am present I will get my treasure, right?"

"Your treasure." The Grasshopper smiled.

"Couldn't we go to the glass island? Right now?"

"To the glass island." The Grasshopper performed a little bow. "I have to warn you, however. There is nothing you can get for yourself from the past. Your treasure, Zzzeldina, will not come to you the way you expect it. It will be a challenge. I cannot tell you how to make it yours. It will be up to you. But I can give you advice: as long as we are traveling in the past, use your little friend as your guide. He is all you can know about the past, all you can reach." Her long, very long hand came over and lightly touched Zelda's left ear. There was a coolness, a faint rustle of leaves. "Do you hear me? Finding a treasure that matters entails a risk, the same way that finding an answer does."

CHAPTER 19

On the glass island, nothing was made of glass. Only shabby little factories and houses that looked like stables. Between them, a small, ugly canal. It was drizzling. There was nothing but mud.

"Eehnuff?" Zelda heard Vittorio shout before she spotted him in the back of a red-tiled shack.

"You eehnuff now?" A grin was painted over his face. He was watching Kidcou leap like a puppy over a terrain speckled with puddles and heaps of dirt. He had mud splattered all over his naked legs, his hands, arms, cheeks. He was bouncing right into the puddles, each time snatching something up that looked like clumps of mud. He was stuffing mud into his pockets. Now he turned to his companion with a triumph in his eyes that Zelda had never seen. He rose, his shorts sagging dangerously under the weight of his pockets. He laughed as he pulled them up with his thumbs.

Bewildered, Zelda went to inspect one of the puddles. The bottom, she saw, was studded with glass. Glass was stuck in the mud like raisins in a muffin. Just enough color was visible to entice a keen eye. When she checked the area more closely she found that every puddle was the same. And even the mounds and flat stretches of dirt between them were filled with glass in the same way. This was the glass island after all.

The treasure seemed inexhaustible. The sparks of color that she made out put her most special days of special omens to shame. She readied herself to dig in when she noticed that Kidcou and Vittorio were headed toward the canal. She reached down to snatch at least one piece. She grabbed empty air and cursed. The Grasshopper had warned her. But why had she been able to touch the cake and eat it? It didn't make sense, unless there was some magical formula. Something she needed to figure out. Fast. She tore herself away. Her guides were already at the canal. If she lost them she might never learn the way to the island.

She settled in Vittorio's boat, as close as she could get to the heap of clumps Kidcou had emptied from his pockets into a net. He was holding the net into the water to clean the mud off while the boat was tuck-tuckering through the canal. She wanted to shout at Vittorio to speed up. The water curled and parted around the net like greedy lips.

It seemed to take forever for the treasure to resurface. She stared and stared … and felt as though she herself were being dragged through the water. The vertigo came on and for an instant she fought it, trying to hold on. But in the next moment her whole person was pulled through the eager mouth of the net.

When she came to, she saw pieces of glass in every shape and every color of the rainbow spread over the dining room table, flooded by light from a candelabra.

"*Splendido*! There's enough for all your friends," she heard Uncle Carlo's purrattle.

She didn't see anyone. All she saw was Kidcou's glittering bounty in front of her. Enough to be shared with everyone but her. The whole family was shouting "Oh"s and "Ah"s, picking out pieces and turning them this way and that against the light. The father was toasting Uncle Carlo with a yellow-dotted doll's cup. He teased the baby on his arm pretending to make her drink. Vittorio strutted in front of his sisters, holding up two crystal splinters like earrings of a prima donna. Nina, or was it Tina, dove under the table, chased by her twin, with what looked like a piece of a candy cane. Each in turn tried her teeth on it. The orange base of a vase turned into a monocle which the grandmother donned. Everyone laughed. She looked like an owl with half of a pair of sunglasses. Kidcou decorated the mother's blouse with the wedge of a crystal daisy, rattling away in Italian.

After a time, the men gathered at the free corner of the table around a bottle of wine. Uncle Carlo puffed on his pipe and kept an eye on Kidcou, smiling occasional "*splendidos.*" The teenager who had pushed the foot of a champagne glass into her teased hair like a flying saucer, brought a tray from the kitchen to gather the treasure up for Kidcou. He went around the room and handed everyone a gift. Again, "*Bello, bellissimo,*" and "*Grazie,*" were shouted, but Nina and Tina made faces to each other about what they got. Zelda saw that the adults dropped their gifts almost as soon as Kidcou turned his back. It was true, heaped onto the tray, away from the light, the glass looked like a simple pile of broken pieces, almost like rubble swept up after an earthquake.

"I don't think they like them," Kidcou said. They were suddenly back in the lab. Kidcou was half-lying on the table, his treasure tray between his arms. "Not really," he added.

The grasshopper in the cage on the same table stirred,

"Gzzz-gzzz-gzzz."

"*He* likes them," Kidcou said, sounding unconvinced. "Uncle Luigi gave me back the piece I gave him as a gift. He said I must keep it for my collection. Nina and Tina just left theirs on the table. And then Concetta threw them in the garbage bin."

"*Non e possibile.*" Uncle Carlo looked up from his microscope.

"*Si si.* When I emptied my egg cup after breakfast, I saw it. I did. At first it looked like real treasure all together. But then nobody found it beautiful anymore. Why?"

"Gzzz-gzzz-gzzz," the grasshopper went.

"Ah," Uncle Carlo scribbled a few notes into a scrapbook. "Your friend here seems to know that it takes special eyes to see. Let's have a look together, you and I." He drew a chair over to Kidcou's table. "Mind you, *la mama* brought me the mail this morning, wearing her orange monocle!"

He picked out a piece and turned it this way and that against the light before passing it on to Kidcou.

"This one for example. A magnificent golden green. If we look at the color alone we can only say, a marvel. Now, if we look at the shape of it, what can we say? It is perhaps an ear — "

"An ear?" Kidcou crinkled his nose. He held the piece to his ear. "And what do we hearrr?" He perfectly imitated his uncle's purrattle.

"*Sacrrrrra!*" Uncle Carlo said it with at least five "r"s. "The lovely cup the glassblower was making, I hear it breaking! *Oi me!* All that's left now is its ear with this little corner of the cup hanging on!"

"Nina and Tina liked this one." Kidcou pretended to lick a striped cane.

"A lollipop? It might have been the stem of a tall wine glass. Perhaps the glassblower wasn't satisfied with the chalice and decided to start over?"

Kidcou considered it.

"We could speculate this way, you see, about most of these pieces. Something was attempted that didn't exactly work out."

"But doesn't this look just like a swan?"

"A swan!" Zelda couldn't help herself. "The spout of a tea pot."

"I once had a swan exactly like it," Kidcou said. "With such light blue lines inside, only it was so thin that nothing was left when it broke. But here much, much is left."

"Enough for our imagination," Uncle Carlo nodded. "*E vero.* Imagination can make a broken swan whole again. With imagination, your treasure is perfect, every piece of it, and it is all yours. Nobody can take it away from you. *Ma* — but, can someone else see it, too, and share it with you? That may be the problem. Someone else might only see what went wrong in the glassblower's workshop. Which pieces came out with major and minor flaws so that he discarded them while he kept only the finest and best."

"I didn't get the finest and best? Only what was thrown away?"

"*Piano, piano* — I wouldn't say that," Uncle Carlo smiled a big cat's smile. "When our eyes are new and fresh, we are unwilling to discriminate, you see? Everything sparkles alike. The next step, then, is to compare and make choices, the way the glassblower did himself. With the eye of the artist who imagines and seeks perfection. You have that eye, *si si.* I see that some pieces of great beauty have already caught your attention."

Zelda quickly scanned the tray. She, too, might have the eye of an artist.

"Can you tell me which is your favorite piece?"

Kidcou went through his basket. He looked and looked, all the while holding on to his teapot "swan."

"This one." He grabbed something before Zelda could make it out. "Nina and Tina both wanted it. I couldn't give it away, Uncle Carlo. I wanted to, but I said no." He passed a blue ball of glass to his uncle who rolled it over his palm.

"*Ecco*! I couldn't more agree. You see, this is a magnificent blue, but that isn't all. If you study the art of glass, you will discover that it resembles a very rare kind of blue. You will find it in the past, hundreds of years back in time, when the gothic cathedrals were built. Glass, back then, around the twelfth, thirteenth century, was rare and precious. Blue glass was even rarer, it was hard to make. But this particular blue was the rarest of all. The artisans who discovered its secret kept their lips sealed. Only those initiated into the art of glassblowing at the little town of Chartres, in France, knew *il secreto*. People from all over the world still come to see the heavenly blue in the windows of the cathedral of Chartres."

"And then?" Kidcou asked.

"The secret that was never told; it was lost over time. Today, with all our modern sciences and technologies, glassblowers are still trying to recreate the blue of Chartres. Do they succeed? *Alora*, this one comes interestingly close."

Kidcou had leaned his head against Uncle Carlo's shoulder. He looked as if he was seeing a world of secrets in the ball of glass. Zelda couldn't resist sneaking up to Uncle Carlo's other shoulder. She always liked a good story. Right then, he readjusted his position, and she almost fit. She couldn't possibly be too tall for the arm of Uncle Carlo's chair.

"If we analyze further," Uncle Carlo inspected the ball of glass with Sherlock Holmes eyes, "we might speculate that the shape has something to do with this particular blue. In the same way that the shape of a musical instrument has something to do with the tone it produces."

Kidcou nodded.

"Here we have an almost perfect sphere, which means a smooth, unbroken surface and a compact depth for the rays of light to play upon, like on a fine instrument. With a little stretch, we could say that this marble gives you the almost perfect music of blue."

Kidcou and his uncle exchanged a knowing look. Blue music? Zelda assumed you had to have perfect pitch in order to hear such a thing.

"*Ecco*. A piece for an artist's collection." Uncle Carlo handed it back to Kidcou. " Usually, blue ranges among the cool colors on the spectrum, as you know from our studies of optical laws. But in this case, the red side of the spectrum seems to shine up from the very center with a bit of violet to warm up the blue sphere. *Molto interressante* ... There are people with eyes like this, do you realize? Your mother. Yourself. A similar blue with a warm shine from deep down. Down from where? One could be bold and say, from the soul."

"What's the soul?" Kidcou asked just before Zelda did.

"There is no easy answer to that."

"But you are a scientist," Kidcou objected.

"Science can't answer all the questions, my boy."

"They haven't found the secret blue, but I see it and I hear it," Kidcou said, his eyes almost the same color as his ball of glass.

A silence fell over the room.

Zelda read the look in Uncle Carlo's eyes. There was a secret meaning to all his talking. A sadness that he kept hidden. Was he teaching Kidcou about the blue to make sure something wouldn't get lost? But it couldn't happen now that she was here. She would figure out a way to save Uncle Carlo. That had to be her purpose. She slapped her invisible forehead. She could have told the Grasshopper right away in the cherry tree!

Uncle Carlo patted Kidcou's head for a moment.

"What about the rest of your treasure?"

"This one?" Kidcou picked up a triangular shard.

"A spectacular yellow, *e certo. Ma* — to be honest, a faint echo of the music."

"Is my swan also only an echo? How can one be sure?"

"Ah, can one be sure? One may be mistaken."

"I had a friend, in Germany, I thought he was my friend. I was so sure but ... how could I know?"

"That he would betray you?"

It took Kidcou a while to answer. "He was a singer, too. Everyone said that he was brilliant. His voice, Uncle Carlo! I thought he must like me, too. We sang together, in concert and all. But then he was so...mean."

"You mistook his brilliant voice for his character, perhaps? *Una confusione interessante* ...You know from observation that a bright light can hide a whole room behind it, don't you? Well, brilliance can be blinding, and it can hide many

195

things, cruelty, for example, or envy."

Uncle Carlo took a piece of cut crystal from Kidcou's tray. "Look here, *guarda*. If I hold this crystal to the light and make its facets sparkle, you may be enchanted, you may not notice its broken edges. Perhaps your friend in Germany had the quality of such a splinter?"

"How can I not be blinded?" Kidcou clutched his "swan" with resignation.

"Next time, you mean? Let me tell you from my own experience that it gets easier with time. Who is your friend, and who isn't, will seem obvious one day." He patted Kidcou's hand. "Because you will have learned to discriminate. You will be able to find the very best in a human being even if it doesn't shine, even if it is carefully hidden."

"Like the grasshopper you found among millions of grasshoppers?"

"*Ecco*, I see you understand."

"How did you find him, Uncle Carlo? How could you tell?"

"Ah, sometimes one could wonder who found whom?" Uncle Carlo smiled his big cat's smile.

"Can't you find me, too?" Zelda leapt off the chair and sent a little breath into his white fluff of hair.

"One senses when something special happens." He lifted his free hand to straighten his hair. "One sometimes feels it like a breath of air."

Zelda tried it on Kidcou.

"I feel it," Kidcou confirmed, stroking his ear.

She bent down to the grasshopper's cage and blew into it. The long antennae waved like the tails of a kite in the sky.

"Your special friend also feels a presence, it seems." Uncle

196

Carlo suddenly looked attentive. "Sometimes talks like this call up good spirits in a room…"

Zelda took cover behind the back of his chair. She had to be careful. If she got called up as a good spirit, she might get stuck in the past and not fulfill her purpose.

Uncle Carlo chose another ball of glass from Kidcou's tray. "How about this one?"

"Oh yes, this one is also my favorite. It's just like your eyes, Uncle Carlo. See? Light brown, with green dots." Kidcou held the two balls up together. "We are looking at each other!"

Uncle Carlo smiled. "And we like what we see."

"I want to make a collection," Kidcou said with determination. "Do you think Vito will take me again?"

"I would take you myself, my boy, if my old pump here didn't give me all this trouble." He tapped on his chest.

"I want it to be a real, real treasure, Uncle Carlo." Kidcou threw his arms around his uncle's neck. "I want it for you!"

CHAPTER 20

Zelda found Kidcou at a table in an unfamiliar room. He was humming and turning a big-bellied glass jar around and around under the shine of a lamp. Her head spun. He had finished his collection.

The jar was filled almost to the brim with perfectly-shaped, smooth crystal balls. They were stacked tightly; little marbles filling in the spaces between larger spheres and ovals. Somehow the colors were stacked, too. A cluster of yellows was framed by all kinds of greens, dark bottle-greens and faded sea-greens. A moss-green ball sat next to an egg of a blue as pale as a winter sky. Another turn of the jar brought a cascade of reds and purples into view, shouldering a small marble in exactly the color of Zelda's favorite dessert, lime jello.

She wanted to throw her arms around the jar to hold onto the dream she saw realized. The treasure of treasures. How had he been able to achieve something this magnificent? He must have gone to the island many times. His hair now reached his collar, a whiter wheat than ever, the bangs hanging into his eyes. He was tanned and glowing. He had spent a whole summer with his collection.

She felt her eyes sting with the wonder of it. So she finally knew what it was that he had lost before he came to America. She could not believe it. She could not bear it. She had to somehow keep it from happening. But how? Was it really

200

possible that Uncle Carlo and the Grasshopper needed her?

All of a sudden, there were the hushed voices of Uncle Carlo's family. She hadn't noticed them coming in. They gathered around her, their heads bent over the jar that Kidcou was slowly turning for them. This time, all of them were impressed. They whispered. Their eyes couldn't get enough of it. The father's hand went over Kidcou's head. "*Bellissimo ... incredibile...*," they murmured. Nina and Tina, who now each sported a braid on her head, had their noses pressed against the glass whenever Kidcou stopped turning the jar. The grandmother pulled her orange monocle from her apron pocket. She knuckled the jar for Kidcou to add her piece to the collection. Kidcou gave her an impish look and slipped it right back into her pocket.

"*Vieni,*" Vittorio finally said in a low voice. "Come, Carlo need *resta.*"

"I just have to let the grasshopper out," Kidcou whispered back.

Before leaving, the family peeked over and around a screen in a corner of the room. There was a bed behind it, Zelda saw. This was Uncle Carlo's bedroom. Kidcou waited until the door was closed, then moved the screen to the side. His uncle opened his eyes with a faint smile.

"Help me, will you? I, too, want to see them again." He looked as white as his hair that had lost its fluff and was sagging on his head. His cheeks were sagging, too. Half of him seemed gone, he was so thin. Kidcou, who was bursting with health, helped him into a terrycloth robe and supported him in a slow passage to the table. Uncle Carlo sank into a chair.

While he recovered his breath, Kidcou opened the grasshopper's cage. It was placed on a small bedside table next to a tray of medicine bottles. The grasshopper leapt out without a moment's hesitation. It went straight to the edge of the jar. With another little hop, it went inside, and now was perched on the blue sphere that crowned the center.

"*Splendido*," Uncle Carlo said after a long moment. "It is achieved. More beautiful than an emperor's jewels."

"You helped me, Uncle Carlo. Without you..."

"I knew you had it in you, my boy." He moved an unsteady hand over to stroke Kidcou's bangs off his forehead and tap a spot between his eyes. "In here, and in here," he tapped on Kidcou's chest, "and now we can all see it and enjoy it. Just as we can hear it when you sing."

Kidcou continued to turn the jar for him. "See here? The one that's like your eyes is right next to my blue one."

"We are still looking at each other? So we will, forever then."

"Forever." Kidcou sealed it.

"A treasure no one can take away from you." Uncle Carlo nodded pensively.

Zelda drew in her breath. He was wrong. She knew the treasure would be taken away from Kidcou. How could Uncle Carlo not know? He had seemed to know everything, but now he didn't?

"It's for you, Uncle Carlo, all for you!"

"For me." Uncle Carlo gave Kidcou a long look. "To make me better?"

Kidcou swallowed.

"Every time I look at it I feel better, don't you know? Crystal, the only pure, geometric structure found in nature. The ancients believed in its power to balance energies, and heal all kinds of ailments..." He took Kidcou's hand. "You've given me many gifts since you came to live here, you know? To see you grow, to hear you sing, laugh, and ha! to see you eat. You make me proud to be your friend."

"Can't you get better for a little while?"

"There are always miracles, my boy. When you went out on that beam in the storm and sang, and then came back with the grasshopper, both of you unharmed, I would say it was a miracle. But this one is not too likely. We had better be prepared. You will need this," he half-raised two fingers to point to the jar of crystals, "to heal your own heart when my old pump here wants to rest. And it deserves its rest, you see. I've coaxed and tricked it longer than you know."

"You are not really, are you, not really … going?" Kidcou almost looked the way he had when he had lost his voice.

Zelda wanted to knuckle her temples to keep it out. There were miracles — Uncle Carlo had said it himself. But someone had to make them happen.

"On my last ride?" Uncle Carlo helped him out. "I have no doubt. My friend here," he nodded to the grasshopper who had leapt to the edge of the table in front of him, "who knows more things than you and I, told me a long time ago."

"Told you?"

"When I was young she let me know in a dream."

"She?" Kidcou looked confused.

"A messenger. A beautiful woman, as they say, who comes to teach us mysteries … Why not?" His eyes were far away, as though he had already left.

Zelda held her breath.

"And the dream?" Kidcou brought him back.

"Ah. In that dream she held up an hourglass for me and

then — " his shaky hand performed the movement, "slowly turned it. That was the dream."

"What did it mean?" Zelda and Kidcou asked in chorus.

"It told me my time was measured. I was thirty-one when I had the dream. Now I am sixty-two. You see? With that turn, I was granted another round. The sand is running out."

"But couldn't it be turned again, just one more time?"

"Just for you, I wish it could. But let me tell you, I have used the second half well. When I was thirty-one, I was already old. Old, not wise. My heart gave me all kinds of trouble even then, and I had concluded life wasn't worth living. A blind fool, you might say." He paused to catch his breath. "But then I found this precious companion of mine, and this, together with the dream I told you, changed my life. I began to understand a few things … " Again he seemed to be far away.

"And now?" Kidcou sounded anxious.

"My work is done. Even though everything still needs to be done. I won't go much further, not in this body at least. I am ready."

"But what about me?" Kidcou suddenly choked. "I am not ready. I can't stand — "

"Yes, my boy. I know, but let me tell you something … " He closed his eyes for a moment. "Life and death … Are they the beginning and the end? Or just different forms — " he held his chest as if fighting a wave of pain. "Where do we come from? Where do we go? These questions make it worth our while to live. To live with passion. That's what I learned … that's what I hoped to give you." His voice betrayed his effort. "You will stand it, for my sake. You will."

"But Uncle Carlo," Zelda jumped in, "I'll find a way!"

He suddenly sank back in his chair. Kidcou helped him back to bed. The grasshopper, Zelda noticed, hopped along like a dog and settled on top of a bedpost. With the faintest gesture, Uncle Carlo waved Kidcou closer.

"The grasshopper — must tell you — " He was hardly audible. His eyes were closed.

"Yes, Uncle Carlo," Kidcou said. "The grasshopper."

" — will help you find — " was all Zelda made out even though she almost bumped her invisible head into Kidcou's, trying to get closer to the faint words.

"Thank you, Uncle Carlo." Kidcou had placed his head on his uncle's chest. "I am so glad to have him."

" — friend for you — " Uncle Carlo brought out.

Kidcou nodded. "Yes, he's my friend … "

Uncle Carlo faintly nodded, then shook his head, trying, it seemed, to say or make Kidcou understand something else. But the movement of his lips didn't produce the words.

Zelda felt she couldn't stand it another minute. Why hadn't he told about the Grasshopper a long time ago, when there was plenty of time to talk? Why had he given Kidcou all those lessons without teaching him what really mattered? What was it about adults that they knew so many things, but the most important things they didn't know or kept a secret? What's wrong with you?, she wanted to shout at Uncle Carlo, but to her surprise she heard herself say,

"Don't worry, Uncle Carlo, I'll tell him. Later."

Uncle Carlo seemed to relax. His jaw sank down a little. He was asleep.

CHAPTER 21

It took Zelda a moment before she noticed the change. Again Kidcou was at the table, staring at the jar in front of him. But Uncle Carlo's bed was empty. Where was he? And why was Kidcou still sitting there?

The door opened and Vittorio stormed in, his hair standing on end, his nose and ears red.

"*Operazione* good, *molto* good," he blurted out.

It must be cold outside. Perhaps it was already winter. Kidcou was wearing his scarf inside the house. His tan was gone. He looked thin and oddly familiar. Zelda's heart skipped a beat. This was how he had looked when he arrived in America.

"There is hope?" Kidcou asked.

Vittorio nodded, tearing up. "I run tell Mama." He must have driven his boat straight from the hospital.

Kidcou waited until Vittorio was out the door. Then he crumpled like a pinched balloon. His forehead ended up on the edge of the table.

"Uncle Carlo, please, please —" he muttered. He fell silent.

Zelda stared at the slump of his back. She wanted to pat him the way his foster mother had. But he wasn't sobbing. She wasn't sure what he was doing.

"Come on, Uncle Carlo will for sure make it," she said, but she didn't believe it any more.

"Grasshopper," she called out, "why don't you do something? Right now! Why can't he know who you are? Why hasn't he been told? Why does everything depend on me? It's not fair!" She wanted to rattle the cage to shake the Grasshopper into action. To shake Kidcou's silence away. What was she supposed to do?

Everything was wrong. Everyone was wrong. Vito was wrong. Uncle Carlo was wrong for not telling Kidcou the secret. And the Grasshopper was wrong for plotting with Uncle Carlo and then suddenly dropping the ball and doing nothing. She felt one of her rages coming on. Just in time, she reminded herself to address the Grasshopper properly, the way she had the first time.

"Grasshopper, Grasshopper," she croaked impatiently, "why don't you show yourself? Can't you see that he needs help?" Maybe that would count as a rhyme? No answer. The insect didn't stir in its cage, just as Kidcou didn't stir from his slump.

"I don't want to watch this. I didn't come with you to Italy for this!" she shouted. Why wasn't Kidcou angry? It would be more bearable to see him kicking and hitting and screaming at everything that wasn't fair. But she could tell just from looking at him that it was no use.

She remembered one thing. When she was at the end of her rope and her anger only made everything worse, she talked to her ally. But how was he supposed to do that? His one true ally, Uncle Carlo, was dying. He had no idea that another ally was locked in that cage, waiting. Perhaps he didn't even know about allies because someone had forgotten to tell him in time.

"You need an ally," she told him. "An ally!"

Kidcou drew up his scarf as if he was feeling a draft. Something was getting to him. But he did nothing. She went on repeating her message. She tried to find a rhyme for "ally." Bully? Silly? To hell with rhymes. At least she had found something to do. She stomped around his table as if it were her cherry tree, her arms curling up and down like waves, her feet tapping the floor of Uncle Carlo's bedroom. Round and round she went. This was what it meant to have a purpose.

Suddenly she noticed a movement in the room. The grasshopper had started walking in a circle, in step with her dance. She had been noticed. Her pulse beat faster. She had made a connection. Something would happen. Now.

She must have bumped her head. Bumped it hard. There was her mother. Zelda's vision was blurred. When she blinked, she bumped into her mother again.

"Holy goat ... " she muttered.

Her mother was sitting at the big dining table with Uncle Carlo's sister and the sister's husband, who for once didn't hold the baby. Someone had betrayed her, Zelda thought. Her mother had come to take her home in triumph. She ducked under the table.

Then it struck her. This wasn't real. It was once again the past and she herself wasn't in it. Just to make sure, she stayed under the table.

They were talking as if they were old friends. Talking in Italian. What on earth was her mother doing here? There was quick banter and laughter, then abrupt silence when the name Carlo came up. The name Elmuto was mentioned. Zelda heard her mother stop and repeat, "Kidcou?"

A long story followed, and Zelda knew exactly how it went.

Her mother shouted, "Oh!," "Ah!," "*Non e possibile*!," just like an Italian. The other names of the family came up as well: Nina, Tina and the rest. Her mother seemed to know them all. And finally Zelda heard the name of her father, mentioned in one breath with her own. There wasn't the least note of alarm in her mother's voice. Her mother must be on one of her trips abroad that Zelda had always resented. She resented it now. Of course, her mother would meddle. She always meddled. In the same way her father always pottered.

Zelda peeked when everyone jumped up and rushed to the door. Kidcou's foster parents entered the room. Had they once again come to take Kidcou away? But where was Kidcou?

She sneaked out of the room and leapt up the stairs to Uncle Carlo's bedroom. It was empty. She checked the lab. Empty, too. And dusty. Nobody had been here in a while. The grasshopper's cage was in its usual spot, however, with the critter inside.

She felt the draft even before the curtain moved. Kidcou was standing at that same window that had blown open in the storm. He was staring out. Was he planning to go out on that beam again? This time to save his uncle? His face was ashen. His eyes were almost black, not blue.

She quickly returned to the dining room. She had to know what was up.

Now only her mother and Kidcou's foster parents were left. Zelda slipped back into her observation post under the table from where she could peek. She was just in time to hear her mother say to Kidcou's foster father, "Yes, we are family, and more than that. You have always wanted the best education for Helmut. Granted. But if you want to give him a musical education, Harald, Venice might do well enough."

"Leave him here, without Carlo?" Kidcou's foster father gave her a curious look. "And we all know now that there is no chance for Carlo's recovery. No, no. I agreed to send Helmut to Venice only because of Carlo. Don't you see — " he lowered his voice, "that the rest of the family is not quite … up to our standard?"

Zelda's mother raised her eyebrows. "It can only be good for a child to see different worlds." Zelda could tell she was getting onto her soapbox. "That's the best education you could wish for. The human education. And these people whom I've also known for quite a while, have their hearts in the right place, believe me. Isn't that what counts? Especially for Helmut?"

"I know, I know," he replied, stroking his little mustache. "Of course, we have nothing against them. It's just that Helmut is losing time. He's already behind for his age. If he went now to an Italian school, he'd fall further back. It wouldn't help his English. And it wouldn't help him fit into the school we have chosen for him. Quite the contrary, I'm afraid."

"Cheats!" Zelda hissed. "Betrayers! You promised not to send him back."

There was a silence. But that didn't mean it was settled. Zelda knew her mother. She never gave up an argument.

"Of course, we are concerned in case he is still not ready for his school … " Kidcou's foster mother was fiddling with the gold chain of her glasses. "Something must have happened there the first time. But we never found out what exactly…"

"They said he was just a tad too young to enroll," her husband cut the topic short.

"And now he is old enough to be thrown back?" Zelda's

mother asked with an edge to her voice.

"A sensitive young mind should not be in a house that is going through painful changes, death and mourning," Kidcou's foster father declared.

Zelda's mother huffed. "Keep him away from death? After he's lost his own parents? Whom he could never mourn because he was too young?"

Zelda drew in her breath with pride before she felt the pang of longing. If only she could hear her mother defend her like that! Once, just once to hear her like that.

"Have you asked Helmut's opinion about it, Harald?"

"He is too young to have an opinion, Ellen. Legally at least, as you know. We have to choose for him."

"Well?"

"No, we haven't told him that he's going back to boarding school. We will, after we've been to the hospital."

Not told him?, Zelda wondered. Why then had Kidcou looked as if he knew?

"I don't envy you your responsibility," her mother said quietly. "What if it backfires?"

Kidcou's foster mother nervously adjusted her rolls and combs.

"It won't backfire," her husband declared. "We'll arrange for the school therapist to take care of that. From the start, this time."

Zelda saw the sad, drooping eyes of that man who never spoke. She saw the whole scene again: the headmaster's hidden threats, the young teacher's embarrassment, the head boy's knife-like eyes. She saw Kidcou waddle like a duck, unable to utter a sound.

"No!" she yelled. "You promised! You promised him not to send him back! Grasshopper, don't let them do it!"

She grabbed the table leg and shook it. The rattle of cups and spoons brought her to her senses as much as the dead silence that followed it.

"What was that?"

"Good God!"

"We must have had an earthquake," Zelda's mother said. "Down in Los Angeles we have them all the time, you know."

"But ... a sea quake?"

Zelda forgot to breathe. She had touched the table leg for real. Any second now, she would be discovered by her unreal mother from the past. The nausea was washing over her. She reached for the glass pebble in her pocket. She could not get it out. She panicked. The scene began to blur.

"Grasshopper!" she cried out. "Make her take him! Make my mother take Kidcou away with her. Right now!"

Just as she was drifting away she heard her mother say,

"Come to think of it." She had the shy, young woman's laugh she got after a glass or two of wine. Her voice was tender. "Ed, you know, he's a man quite a bit like Carlo ... "

CHAPTER 22

Zelda was rushing through the house. She hadn't taken notice before, but she seemed to be able to get around even when doors were closed. She only had to want to be in a certain room, and there she was. It seemed natural and now that she thought about it, a bit uncanny, as if she were willing the course of her own boat. She had heard her mother's proposition; she was approaching the present — and it suddenly seemed too fast. How many more leaps before she would hit the present? Would there be time left to look for her treasure?

She urgently needed to keep track of things — how Uncle Carlo was doing, what was going to happen to Kidcou. She flew through the basement with its line of rubber boots on the bench, up the stairs, into the kitchen where Concetta was baking biscotti with the twins, and on through the hallway into Uncle Carlo's lab. Something brought her to a halt.

Kidcou was back in his usual position, half-lying on the table. His arm was touching the treasure jar. At his side, in Uncle Carlo's arm chair, sat Zelda's mother. She had the attentive look that told Zelda she was waiting to make her move.

"It must have been quite a lot of work to put this together," she said. "What an amazing collection."

"An emperor's jewels. My Uncle Carlo said." Kidcou didn't look at anything.

"Yes, Carlo always knew how to find the right words for something special."

Their eyes locked for a second. The shock in Kidcou's, face made Zelda aware that her mother had used the past tense.

"I never knew your parents," her mother moved forward. "But I knew Carlo very well. We worked together, in the old days. A committee of lawyers, like myself, and scientists. One of the many international efforts to save Venice from drowning. He told you about the problems of the sinking city?"

"I know. He showed me," Kidcou said in a toneless voice.

"I used to come to Italy every year, and we got along, he and I and the whole family. It will be — " she considered for a second, "strange now — "

"Did he have this grasshopper already?"

"He always did seem to have some grasshopper around, come to think about it."

"He first met the grasshopper in France, he told me."

For a moment, Zelda's mother had a slightly alarmed look on her face.

"In France, eh? Well, it's true, Carlo always was an eccentric. He claimed that he had talks with nature, with a tree, let's say. Or grasshoppers. They allegedly gave him his scientific ideas. We used to make fun of him, and he would laugh with us and say, '*Oi me*, you are all so rational, and so proud of it! How proud you are of missing the essential, the mysteries.'"

"Mysteries?"

"Well, what can't be explained or understood rationally. For example, why we all have to die and why some of us die too young."

"He almost saved Venice, didn't he?"

She smiled. "His ideas were not quite ... realizable. At least, back then. To support them statistically would have required large experiments with wind and water, tides and floods, and even plants, algae and such. That couldn't be financed, so people were never convinced. Some believed in his visions, most did not.

"He told you, didn't he? By now some of his ideas have been proved realistic enough. But he used to be quite philosophical about it. He would joke that his grasshopper knew more than all of us together!"

"You bet!" Zelda said between her teeth.

Kidcou nodded as if this went without saying. "He's special," he declared.

Her mother pursed her mouth. "And you and the grasshopper are special friends, I hear. Well, you may become his guardian ... for good." She and Kidcou exchanged another look. "So, we both know what there is to be faced. And I want to ask you a question. In case you cannot stay here, in Italy, do you want to go back to the boarding school in England? Do you like that idea?"

She had to repeat her question. Kidcou stared at her.

"Uncle Carlo didn't want to go to the hospital," he burst out. "He needs me, I know he does."

"And he needs *me*!" Zelda jumped in. "He needs me just as much."

"He told you? About the hospital?"

"Just before they took him. He said he knew it was no use. He wanted to stop them. He didn't want it at all, at all."

"I see. He wanted to stay here, at home. In peace. Perhaps he was right. We know now that the operation only proved his point. I'll tell you what. I'll talk to the family and to his doctor. I'll do what I can."

Now Kidcou didn't turn his eyes away from her. "When?"

"Today. Right after we've talked, okay? I promise. What I need to hear from you is whether you want to go back to that school, given the choice. It's important. You need to tell me the truth."

His eyes suddenly flashed with life.

"Never!" he almost shouted. "I'll never never go back there! Never!" For a moment, he had the same fierce look as her mother. Zelda cheered with her fist.

"I understand." Her mother stroked his head for a second, and Zelda started as though she herself had been touched. "Perhaps it won't be necessary. We are all trying hard to find a solution. Everyone here will feel lonely without Carlo, perhaps you most of all. You've already been through a lot for your age. I wanted to mention to you that I have a girl, in California, and she is lonely, too."

Zelda cringed. Who was she talking about? A girl? Lonely? This was the dreaded moment. She, Zelda, was showing up in the past. She was being shown up by her mother. And her mother was making it up to rope him in.

"Her name is Zelda. She is older than you, but she still wants to believe she is a child."

What had she done to deserve this?

"It's a fixed idea of hers. At any rate, she's too much in a world of her own and it worries her father and me. Because otherwise Zelda is a person with an excellent mind and a big heart. She's very popular at school, good at sports and math, she's a passionate reader and explorer, and she's got a head full of red curls." Her mother had emptied her bag with one shake.

Kidcou walked his fingers up and down the glass jar, non-committal.

"I sometimes wish," her mother went on, "she weren't always alone at home, left to her wild ideas. I wish I could find a companion for her, someone to help her out."

Help her out? Zelda couldn't believe her ears. She was the one who was going to help people and make a difference.

"And share her stories," her mother added. "I fear she has too much imagination. She's got her pals at school, but she doesn't have a real friend. I'm always too busy. Ed, her father, is busy, too. He tries very hard to be her friend — " She paused, pursing her lips. "Young people should stick to each other, that's only natural. But he's a man quite a bit like Carlo, you know. Always studying nature, philosophy, the stars, birds ... "

"Does he have a grasshopper, too?"

"There are lots of crickets in the garden. And there are hummingbirds."

"Birds that hum?"

"Birds that hover in the air like helicopters, you know."

"*Kolibris*," Kidcou's eyes lit up. "They don't live here. What color are they?"

"Ed would be able to tell you exactly. They are so tiny and fast you can hardly see them."

"Especially when you never stop to look at them," Zelda threw in.

"We have swallows," Kidcou said. "They are fast! Do you have swallows?"

"For sure, and blackbirds, and even eagles."

Zelda humphed. Her mother could hardly tell a blackbird from a swallow, and here she was talking like an expert.

"Well, it's Ed who knows about birds, not I," her mother admitted. "There is always sunshine where we live. You almost never have to wear a sweater. And there's the ocean and — "

"And *Kolibris?*"

Zelda could already see him fussing with his hummingbirds.

"Yes, and all kinds of flowers. Ed grows everything in the garden, and rare orchids in his greenhouse. He studies them. I think you would like him." Zelda's mother gave him another smile. "And you'd like Zelda. She's such an unusual and creative person. A hothead, too, I can't deny that. We have our fair share of disagreements."

"Fights," Zelda corrected. "Yelling, throwing, banging, shouting, screaming. You really want him to have a fair share of that?" Why on earth had she told the Grasshopper to let her mother take Kidcou home with her?

"But we are also very fair in our disagreements. We don't hold back the truth." Her mother paused. Her face suddenly looked sad. "I can't say that I always understand my daughter."

"Then how will you understand him?" Zelda pounced at her. "You don't even know him. You have no idea how scared he can get. He even lost his voice. Next he'll lose his whole treasure, and if I don't stop him, who will? Not you!"

Her mother seemed to have second thoughts. Not being sure made her look vulnerable and young. "Someone my daughter's age would understand her better," she said as if to herself. "That way, I, too, would perhaps learn ... "

Zelda wanted to shut her up. She knew what her mother's

voice could do. How it could sneak into one's chest and crack one's toughest resolves. Now it had sneaked into Kidcou.

Kidcou looked at her. For the first time, he seemed to fully take her in.

"You think I could maybe help?"

His eyes were doing their trick, Zelda saw. They were darkening, blueing in that special way that nobody could resist. Like the eyes of his mother in the silver frame. Like the secret blue in the cathedral Uncle Carlo had been talking about.

And now her mother couldn't look away again.

"Stop it!" Zelda yelled at her. "Don't do that to him! I can't stand it!"

But her mother held his gaze. Her eyes welled up. Her lips parted.

"Stop that swooning!" Zelda threw herself between them in a fury. "You'll never have time for him, never again. He won't understand why we get so mad. He'll be scared of me. He'll be lonely. He's not cut out for us. Don't you see?"

CHAPTER 23

There wasn't a sound. The lab was deserted, the curtains blowing. Zelda bent out the window. No boat. Everyone was gone. Had she been left behind in the past, all alone? She scanned the small canal. How would she get a boat to get out of there?

She must be dreaming. There was a hand creeping out over the cast-iron balustrade of the furthest window in the lab. That hand was familiar. It was hanging limply in the air. Without warning, it let a bright red glass marble drop into the canal.

Zelda was over there in a flash. Kidcou was sitting on the floor behind the blowing curtain, hidden away. The cage with the grasshopper stood at his feet. He had emptied the jar into a heap between his legs, and the heap was only a miserable half of what the jar had held. He was throwing out his treasure. Throwing it out the window. Throwing it away.

Where was the family? Why was he alone? Had they forgotten him? Her mother, of course, was never there when she was needed. Something had gone wrong. Very wrong. *She* had gone wrong. Even she. How could that be? She squinted hard as she saw the next marble fall and disappear.

"Kidcou!" she shouted. He was sitting like a rag doll, not moving an inch. The color had gone out of his eyes. A greyish-blue emptiness was all that was left.

"Must. Must. Must," he muttered.

He was hardly looking at his treasure. He didn't want to look. But she saw. Piece by piece it went: golden, snake-green, winter-blue. Even the one the color of lime Jello.

"Grasshopper! Stop him!" she yelled into the cage. "He's giving up again. He's losing it."

"Everything," he said in a voice that was plaintive and dead at the same time.

"No," she shouted at him. "This won't save Uncle Carlo! Don't give your whole treasure away!"

"Must," he repeated like a broken toy.

"Shut up!" she shouted.

He was fighting off what she was saying. The grasshopper was cowering in a corner of the cage, motionless. The critter looked pushed against the wall. As if they were both pinning it down with equal strength.

"Don't let him lose everything!"

"Everything," Kidcou repeated. The faint *plop, plop*, of glass hitting the water left no doubt about who was winning the argument.

It made her so mad she tried to grab his wrists and wrench the treasure away from him. She had been able to touch and eat the chocolate. She had rattled the table leg. Why couldn't she do it now? There had to be some way to push through to him. She wrestled her invisible body into a sweat.

"I hate you!" she yelled at the grasshopper. "I hate being here. I hate not being here. I hate it all." She knuckled her temples, but she still heard the *plop, plop*, the little splashes of water deep down.

There were hardly any pieces of crystal left on the floor.

"Uncle Carlo would stop you if only he could. Grasshopper, how can I stop him?"

Kidcou seemed to be hesitating. He was holding the last two pieces in his hands.

Zelda's throat was dry. She couldn't have shouted if she had wanted to. The last two. His favorite pieces. The blue ball and the golden hazel one. The color of Kidcou's eyes, and the color of Uncle Carlo's.

Now he looked up. He held the two crystal balls up as though imagining two eyes looking at each other. His lips moved, but no words came. He and Uncle Carlo were looking and talking to each other. And then his upper body turned toward the window. His two fists slowly reached over the balustrade. He closed his eyes and let them drop.

Zelda leapt.

Her leap joined the flock of swallows that dove past the window to the water in a single scream, at the same moment.

CHAPTER 24

She fell and floated, floated and fell.

When she came up again, she was drifting near a checkered fleet of boats on a canal: motorboats, ferry boats, gondolas. In the midst of the commotion, one boat caught her attention. Two men were rowing it, one standing at each end, draped in black capes, with black broad-rimmed hats. Zelda knew it was the boat that comes for the dead. Its center was built up like an altar to hold the coffin that was covered by a black velvet blanket with a silk fringe at the seams. A bouquet of white calla lilies was lying on the coffin.

She recognized the small canal into which the rowers steered, pushing against the walls with their oars. The family was gathered in the open front door, in their rubber boots, dressed in black. The mother and grandmother were holding each other, their heads covered by veils. Nina's and Tina's bright yellow boots stood out like painted toy soldiers in a cemetery. Concetta had her hands on the twins' shoulders. Vittorio and his father, the baby basket at their feet, were staring straight ahead, defying the redness in their eyes. Zelda's mother, wearing a hat, was right behind Kidcou whose face swam like a white buoy on a sea of black. They were waiting for the boat to take Uncle Carlo for his last ride.

The scene was gliding away into the distance. He had died.

228

He had died. Zelda couldn't stand it. All her plans had gone wrong. She had failed. She wanted to go under. Disappear.

But something was carrying her on. She was in a boat. Waves were lapping against the hull. She felt the cool night air. Her boat was moving by itself. She felt it pull around a corner into a dark canal.

The canal was a long, deep pit. The walls towering to the right and left were as old as the world. On the left, a palace looked down at her with ornate windows, statues and columns. On the right, the black holes of a prison were yawning out of the forbidding wall.

A bridge with two windows came into view, linking the two sides of the narrow canal like a passage between life and death.

Zelda's boat stopped.

On the other side of the bridge, another boat was blocking the canal. Turned sideways, the bird-like neck of a gondola was gently bobbing on the water. Zelda strained her eyes against the night. Against the sheen of water, she made out the shape: a tall, slender figure standing in a boat. The figure seemed to be wearing a long water-green gown, but it could also be a cape or a raincoat. Zelda grabbed the Grasshopper's glass pebble from her pocket. There was no sound, just the lapping of water. The night air was still. The Rower was waiting.

The Rower's boat turned and began to move away. Zelda's boat followed as she knew it must. Everything was familiar, everything was unknown. The Rower was gliding ahead. Serene, not touching the oar, she was willing the course of her boat, the course of the night.

Zelda squeezed her eyes shut when her boat moved in under the bridge with its eery windows staring at her. When she blinked again, one boat-length separated her from the Rower's boat. Zelda struggled to steady her hand. The Rower stood in the stern, motionless, waiting. She had been pulling in what was hers. She had been pulling Zelda in ever since Zelda first saw her in the alleys.

"Now she will turn," Zelda tried to prepare herself. "She will turn and look at me."

Slowly she saw the white oval of a face, the shadows of a pair of eyes. A child's face was looking at her with eyes as large and deep as the sea. Zelda's glass pebble dropped from her hand into the water.

The Rower's face came closer. Now it seemed to consist of nothing but eyes. Zelda wondered whether she was looking at the Grasshopper. Was this another secret? The Rower and the Grasshopper were the same? Any moment now the eyes would grow and grow and blow her away. But she was held in a place between terror and an unnameable hope. The Rower, with her strangely huge sloe-eyes, was inviting her in.

Zelda felt fire and ice enter her bones. There was something she recognized in these eyes. There was the color blue as if Kidcou's mother, the woman in the silver frame, were looking at her. There was golden amber, as if Uncle Carlo were looking at her.

She is telling me she has them, Zelda knew. The last of the treasure. Kidcou's most precious pair. She knew it with a wild joy. The Rower was guarding them. And the Rower was the Grasshopper.

"Give them to me," she heard herself say. "I'll do anything.

I mean it. Anything."

She felt the shock of water splashing, the mass of water pressing against her body. She saw Kidcou's blue and gold balls of glass sinking below her. She hunted after them. She got close enough to grasp them. They slipped through her fingers. Soon they would hit the ground, the old stone of the sunken city. She would catch up with them. But the crystal balls didn't stop.

"Grasshopper, give them to me!" she shouted.

The ground of the city gave way, letting her in.

She tried to scream, but the rushing of a strong wind pressed the scream back into her throat. Her body was weightless, falling away. She felt her fear falling away. Her arms spread out. She was going to meet the present. She was ready.

What had been promised was now going to be fulfilled.

PART IV

THE WAY HOME

CHAPTER 25

Zelda was falling backwards through the world. There were bridges, aching with age, bending over lazy roads of water. There were islands of glass, spilled like a handful of crystals over the blue tablecloth of the sea. There were trains worming their way through quilts of yellow, rust, dun. There was sky, night blue, snow blue, Indian blue sky. There were branches, a tree. The bark was smooth. A bump. Warm dirt.

"Aiii!" The pain in Zelda's ankle stung her awake. She had fallen from a tree. The cherry tree. In her own garden. She squinted at the house. It must be early morning. A few jays were bickering in the neighbors' fig tree. Nobody was around.

She rubbed her eyes. She pinched herself. Was she back where she had started? Had she ever left? Where was the Grasshopper?

Alarmed, she hobbled over to the juniper hedge. There was the cage with the grasshopper inside. Kidcou was crouching over it. In his pajamas. He looked dazed.

"You scared the ship out of me," he growled at her. "Where did you hide my grasshopper? I looked everywhere. In your room, in the greenhouse, everywhere."

"What do you mean? You rummaged through my room?" She stopped herself. Her heart skipped a beat. The grasshopper had been gone. Her adventure hadn't been a dream.

She hadn't made it up. She struggled to keep her mind steady.

"I didn't hide a thing. I told you. I left you a note."

"It's not fair. It's mean what you did. It's cruel. How could you take my grasshopper away?"

"You don't understand. I didn't mean to — " She suddenly felt sheepish. How long had she been away? How long had he been searching, waiting?

"I didn't take the grasshopper. The grasshopper took me. Because I discovered the secret. It's not a he, by the way. It's a she."

Kidcou glowered at her. "I never told you that. I wanted a he-hopper, and my Uncle Carlo didn't mind."

"You knew? What else did you know?"

"Who cares! I don't talk to you." He turned his back to her and bent over the cage again, pressing his nose against the wire. Zelda had a flash of him hugging the cage on the beam over the canal, after the grasshopper had returned to safety.

"I like the grasshopper too," she said. "I brought her back. From Italy." Kidcou seemed to ignore her. "Yeah, Venice. Uncle Carlo's house. I've been there. With Nina and Tina and everyone." She saw him freeze. "I even heard you sing at that big church in Vienna, before the telegram arrived."

He turned to look at her as though she had lost her mind.

"It's true. I saw the train. And Mark, I saw how he popped that marble into his sleeve. That rat. And you gave him forty-eight marzipan breads!"

"Never! Who told you such lies?" He rose up in a flash, red to his ears.

"I saw you. I saw what happened at the boarding school, how you made a fool of that mean carrot-head and got yourself kicked out." She raised her elbows and waddled on the spot, shouting at his disbelief, "Quaaak! Quaaak! Quaaak!"

He turned pale as if he were back in that room with the four beds.

"It was the greatest," she reassured him. "You blew my mind. And, boy, was he impressed. They all were. They couldn't get you, ha? They tried, but they couldn't."

She saw his confusion, his helpless glance at the grasshopper in the cage.

"I just followed you — with the Grasshopper who isn't a grasshopper at all. Not really."

"I don't believe you. The grasshopper is my special friend. He would never betray me."

"Betray you?" She was spilling his secrets in the worst kind of way. "The Grasshopper hasn't said a thing about you." That wasn't true. How could she explain it?

"I didn't mean to spy," she tried. "I just wanted to get out of here. But when I set the Grasshopper free, we had to follow you around to Italy." She could see she wasn't making any sense. "The Grasshopper came here with you, so we had to take the same way you had taken. We followed you into the past, you see?"

"If that was true, my grasshopper would have let me come, too. He would never leave me behind. Never!"

It suddenly didn't seem fair. Was it possible? The Grasshopper, unfair?

"The Grasshopper must have wanted me to see something I couldn't see any other way, I guess. What happened, back then. What you went through. I didn't want to know. So she made me." That sounded true. "The Grasshopper had a purpose.

238

I told you. I had to tag along with you all the way to the present."

"That's bullship," he scoffed. "Why would you do that? You just asked your mom about Nina and Tina and all."

"I didn't. Don't be such a blockhead!" She reminded herself to keep her anger in check. "My mom wasn't on the train with you and Mark, and she wasn't at the boarding school."

"You are just making up stories. Like saying you were found in the garbage. I don't want to listen." He turned to the cage again, his back stiff.

He was right. But this wasn't a story. How could she prove it? Telling him more about what she had seen would only spill more of his secrets. He'd refuse to believe her. Nobody would believe her. Now that he had his grasshopper back, he had eyes only for the critter. Zelda was a fool. Standing there with a tall story and no proof.

She looked at her own hands hanging empty, her same old T-shirt, Bermudas, tennis shoes, her same old self. Hadn't she changed? Didn't it show? She'd been away for what felt like years. Nothing to her was the same, but everything between them was. She might just as well never have gone. Had she messed it all up in the end?

She kicked the dirt, shoved her hands into her pockets, and turned away. So what if nobody believed her? Why should she care? She didn't need them. She knew what she knew. To hell with the rest.

Her fists hit something hard in her pockets. Something that shouldn't be there, that hadn't been there before. She felt the shock of coolness, roundness. Her hands knew before she grasped them.

"Holy goat!" she exclaimed. The crystal balls. She had jumped after them, and now she had them. It was true then. She had found them in the eyes of the Rower who was in fact the Grasshopper. This was what the Grasshopper had been secretly preparing with Uncle Carlo. Zelda felt her mind leaping. She had been part of their plot, perhaps from the first moment the Rower appeared to her.

She must have had a wild look to her as she held out her hands with the two perfect spheres of crystal in them. Kidcou's eyes widened. She saw terror in them, disbelief, scorn. He stared at her. Again, her mind was leaping. He refused to believe her. All the times she'd tricked him and let him down.

"For you," she managed to say, her voice grating like the Grasshopper's. "They are yours."

He took a step backwards. His arms went behind his back.

"I jumped in, after you threw them into the canal. I fished them out. The canal with the beam that you climbed on to save the grasshopper from the storm." She wondered if he was even listening, he tried so hard not to look at his gems. "I think the Grasshopper did it all for you. She and Uncle Carlo. They had it all planned. They didn't want you to lose everything. So they sent me after you. To get them back."

Were there no words for what she knew? The blue and golden crystal marbles lay in her hands. They had been given to her to save. But they were getting lighter, their colors thinner by the minute. If Kidcou didn't believe her, if she couldn't convince him, the last of his treasure would be lost. It would disappear forever.

"I couldn't stand that you should lose everything," she pleaded. "Take them."

He still wouldn't move.

"Kidcou!" she shouted. "Do you want to lose them again? Grab them! They are your very last ones. The ones you and Uncle Carlo loved!"

His scorn cracked. He searched her eyes. His hands came forward. Then his gaze turned to wonder. Carefully, as if the marbles were alive, he took them from her hands. He held them up the way he had at the window before he let them fall. Then he bent over them with his whole body, down on his knees. He hugged them to his chest, hiding his face on the ground.

"I'll be right back," Zelda mumbled. She, too, had to hold on to something. She hobbled over to the cherry tree and threw her arms around it. It wasn't enough to squint as hard as she could. She had to hold on tight to bear the shaking that overcame her. It sent her through pain, through crazy laughter, and back. Finally, she let go of the tree. She shook herself. There was no doubt, she was back. In the present. Her mind was clear. There was no doubt about anything.

When she returned to the hedge, Kidcou was lying on the ground, looking at the sky through one, then the other, of his crystal balls. He saw her arrive and rolled over like a puppy.

"Tell, tell, Zeldi! Tell me everything."

CHAPTER 26

The sun was coming up. The shadow from the juniper hedge crept toward Zelda and Kidcou who were lying on their stomachs. She was talking, he listening, marveling at his blue and golden marbles. Another shadow approached.

"Zelda?" Her mother held her briefcase in one hand, a half-eaten muffin and a mug in the other. She must be running late. "Do you guys know how late it is? You should have left for your field trip an hour ago, Zelda. Look at you. Have you slept in your clothes? And you, still in pajamas, Kidcou? What's going on here?"

Kidcou hid his treasure as fast as a squirrel. But her mother had taken it all in, in one split second, Zelda realized. Her mother had recognized the crystal marbles from Kidcou's jar. He had claimed they were lost but in fact, he was just keeping them a secret. Zelda winked at her mother. Sometimes it was best to let parents believe they understood everything.

"We decided to take a day off," Zelda explained, very matter of fact. "For Kidcou, it's basically just sports today, and my field trip … well, after our last big fight we figured we had something important to talk over."

"I see." Her mother pursed her mouth, drawing conclusions with her usual speed.

"I know I should have told you. But it couldn't wait." Zelda helped her mother with another wink. "I think you'll be pleased with the result." From the corner of her eyes she saw that Kidcou was impressed.

Her mother bent her head as though her ear was tingling. Her eyebrows went up. "The result being, I presume, that you have decided to grow up?"

"How about — " Zelda tossed a stalk of grass in the air, "eight going on fifteen?"

"Eight plus eight is sixteen!" Kidcou shouted.

Her mother walked to her car and turned back for one more look. There was respect and amusement in her face.

Zelda waited until the car door banged shut. "The Grasshopper told me that one has to stay forever eight years old in order to become wise."

"Now, now." It was her father. "The voice of wisdom speaking so early in the morning?"

Against the light, she thought for a second the person with the garden apron was Uncle Carlo. Kidcou ran up to her father and took his hand. "We have permission to stay in the garden the whole day. We are working things out."

"How else could it be? I always told you, my daughter is someone to reckon with." He made his eyebrow tufts dance. "After all, she comes from a most distinguished father."

"Dad," Zelda wailed. "I give up. What happened to your glasses?"

The frame stuck out of his apron pocket. He pulled it out.

"Someone left them lying in my chair. I sat on them." He wiggled the broken-off legs between his fingers.

Kidcou nudged Zelda. She nodded.

"I think we can fix them," Kidcou said.

"Can you now?" Zelda's father looked from one to the other. "Then I won't stand in your way." He went to water the potted geraniums on the terrace while Zelda sped into the house to get yarn and a pair of scissors.

"Damn it." The yarn split and wouldn't go through the tiny holes. "We need a needle. Dad, do we have a sewing needle in the house?"

"Fine, medium, thick, or for leather?"

"No need," Kidcou stopped them. "I know how he did it," he whispered. He disappeared into his room and came back with a candle and matches. "With a needle, it gets too thick." He lit the candle, dipped the tip of the yarn into the melted wax and stroked it until the tip was stiff. "Now." He threaded each leg to the frame and tied the knots. He held the scissors to the threads. "This long?" He snipped four times.

Zelda called her father over to try them on.

"A new man is born," he declaimed. "He's not the greatest sight, but he can see."

"You never looked better, Dad." Zelda and Kidcou exchanged a look. "In return, will you promise us something?"

"Promise you?"

"Never to wear them any other way?"

"We love the way it looks," Kidcou affirmed.

"Whatever you say," he chuckled. "As long as the two of you can stand to agree."

CHAPTER 27

Zelda and Kidcou were still lying in the afternoon shade of the juniper hedge when her mother came home.

Zelda called out, "You on strike or something?"

Her mother approached with her briefcase. "Pretty close," she smiled. "I guess I needed a break. There are some pizzas in the car. I hope you don't mind not having to cook tonight. We could do a pizza picnic in the garden. If you two could spread out a couple of blankets and roll the umbrella over? Ed's in the greenhouse, I suppose. Why don't you ask him to pick a nice bottle of red wine to go with the pizza?"

Zelda and Kidcou prepared the picnic on her father's one proud area of grass to the side of the greenhouse.

"Funny," Zelda said. "We haven't had a picnic in a hundred years. What's the matter with her? She never comes home this early." She sat down next to the blanket and slung her arms around her knees. "Do you suppose she's picked up on something?"

"I like picnics," Kidcou sat down, too. "Let's ask her."

She gave him a look. "You ask."

"Tell me again what happened when you jumped from the window."

"Again? Okay, I remember I saw the boat come for Uncle Carlo. So I knew he was dead ... "

They were interrupted by her parents arriving with a picnic

basket, a tray, and a large plate of pizza.

"Is there a reason for another celebration?" Zelda's father opened the bottle of wine.

"I had the impression Zelda and Kidcou had something important to settle today," Zelda's mother said. "I can't say what it is, exactly. But I have a sense that it might ... " She gave a little shrug. Zelda was surprised to see her mother grope for a word and suddenly look sheepish.

"That we made up?" she tried to help out.

"Hmm ... perhaps there won't be as much fighting anymore around here?" It sounded hesitant. The look she gave Zelda was shy.

"Who am I gonna fight with, then?" Zelda managed a mean-eyed stare. As if by secret agreement, everyone turned to her father. He peered back at them over the rim of his glasses with a dangerous scowl that still needed some practice.

"You should have seen the judge who presided over my case yesterday," Zelda's mother laughed. "He'd be worth any drop of fighting you've got in you, Zelda. You should come down to court with me one of these days and see for yourself ... "

"Maybe Zelda should take the whole baseball team to court to join in the fight." Her father's eyebrows leapt up and down.

"I'll come too!" Kidcou shouted.

"You? With a baseball bat?" Zelda sent him a probing squint from the corner of her eyes.

"You bet!" He looked back at her, managing his first good mean-eyed stare.

She grinned. "Reason to celebrate," she summed it up.

"Yes, celebrate!" Kidcou exclaimed. "We celebrate —?" He turned to Zelda.

"Dad's new glasses," Zelda proposed. "Mom, doesn't he remind you of somebody?"

"Dear me." Her mother looked at her husband's glasses with their bits of yarn raised like antennae.

"We did it. Zelda and I," Kidcou explained.

"Well then..." She pursed her mouth, holding back something. "Let's drink to the memory of a dear friend, Kidcou's Uncle Carlo."

"He had glasses just like yours," Kidcou whispered to Zelda's father while he poured a tiny bit of wine for Kidcou and Zelda.

"To Uncle Carlo!" They all clinked their glasses.

"I was never fortunate enough to meet him," Zelda's father said. "But I have heard a lot about him. Apparently some of his ideas for saving Venice have been tested recently and will be put to use, after all."

Kidcou nodded proudly.

"It's too bad he isn't there to see it happening," Zelda's mother said.

"He probably knew anyway," Zelda replied. "I bet his grasshopper told him."

Her mother gave her a funny look. "It's true, he always maintained that it would only be a question of time."

"Perhaps next year, we can all go together and see it with our own eyes," her father said. "Ellen will have to go back to Italy for work, and we could join her for a big family meeting over there. What do you think?"

"To Venice?" Kidcou's eyes were wide. "With Vito and everyone?"

"Your foster parents and everyone. And you will be our guide and show us around," Zelda's mother smiled.

"I could show you a few things, too. The bottom of a canal, for example," Zelda threw in. Kidcou giggled.

Her mother shook her head, amused. "So you like the idea."

"Mom, the last time you were in Italy was just before Uncle Carlo died, right? Did you arrive in time to talk to him? I mean, did you talk about what would happen to Kidcou if Uncle Carlo died?"

Her mother dropped her piece of pizza onto the blanket. "Well, no." She wiped the blanket. "He was already in a coma when I… Are you wondering, Zelda, how the idea of inviting Kidcou to America came up?"

While her mother was finishing with the blanket, Zelda nudged Kidcou. "I thought perhaps it was his foster parents' idea?"

Her mother drew up one knee. She was watching her daughter.

"As far as I remember, a day or two ago, you didn't even know that Kidcou had foster parents," she said. "You must have learned a lot in a few hours."

"Let's say, a few years: from Vienna to England to Italy and back. England wasn't too good an idea though. So whoever came up with America was pretty brilliant, I'd say." Zelda busied herself pouring the juice.

"If you think so," her mother said, puzzled, "I'd have to agree."

"Look, look!" Kidcou pointed to two hummingbirds chasing each other from his feeder in the peach tree. A second later, the chase was repeated at another feeder.

"It looks like they are playing a teasing game," Zelda's father peered over his glasses.

"They fight," Kidcou said excitedly. "They are very territorish."

251

"Territorial," Zelda's father corrected.

"You said they never came to your feeder," Zelda objected. "When that bird fell onto the roof, remember? And now they are suddenly territorish over your feeders?"

"Because I have made for them a territory," Kidcou pointed to a patch of flowers, a trellis, and bushes in full bloom. "Only they didn't know it yet. Your dad helped me plant all the flowers they like. I put oil on the feeders so the ants can't get to them. And now I only keep the sugar water for four days so it doesn't ferment." He looked at Zelda's father to make sure he had said it correctly.

"Unbelievable," Zelda's mother said. "I never noticed this spot in the garden."

Zelda was baffled, too. "It always looks like you'll give up, but then you get there in the end!"

"Quite an insight..." Zelda's mother said. She rose to look at Kidcou's flowers. Everyone followed.

"Salvia, sage, honeysuckle and trumpet vine — they love red flowers — fuchsias, larkspur," Kidcou pointed.

"Congratulations, Kidcou. I wouldn't even know their names. You'll have a lot to show to your foster parents when they come to visit in December."

"They are coming here?" Zelda was alarmed. "What for? They aren't gonna take him away again?"

There was a long silence. Zelda's mother went back to her place on the blanket and took a sip of wine. Zelda kneeled down right in front of her.

"Mom! You stopped them once! You aren't going to allow them to send him back to that disgusting boys' school, are you?"

Her mother gave her a long, searching look. Then she turned to Kidcou. "Well, it will be up to you, Kidcou, to decide if you prefer to go back with them, won't it?"

Kidcou seemed glued to his territory. "I need to plant columbines, red ones. And a butterfly bush," he muttered.

Zelda leapt up again. "I won't let them!" She stomped. "I won't let them send him away again!"

Her mother was silent. Everyone was waiting for Kidcou.

"I can't leave them now…" He shook his head. "I have to take care of my hummingbirds."

Zelda felt her mother grab her arm and squeeze it hard.

"Ouch!" She cried out happily. She punched the air with her fist.

"Oh, there's one at your feeder, over there!" her mother exclaimed like a young girl.

"And he knows what he's doing," Zelda's father observed. "He's only hovering and stealing a few sips to provoke his pal to chase him."

Kidcou gave him a knowing look. He settled back on the blankets with everyone else.

"Why do you say 'he' about the hummingbird, Dad?" Zelda asked. "We always thought the grasshopper was a he. But I found out it's a she."

"I'm impressed." He took her hand.

"How did you do that?" her mother wanted to know.

Zelda decided not to pull her hand away. "Let's see. I had a long talk with the critter one day. Then I double-checked with Uncle Carlo. He said, 'A she? The grasshopper a she? But of course, my dear.'" She perfectly imitated Uncle Carlo's purrattle. "'Even our little blond friend secretly knows that. And that's sufficient scientific proof, if you ask me.'"

Her parents burst out laughing. Kidcou looked shocked and delighted.

"I told you," Zelda's father said, "I am the proud father of a daughter to be reckoned with."

Her mother's eyes were fond and a bit red from the wine. "And I told you, Ed. To come up with a story like that, you have to be eight years old for quite some time."

CHAPTER 28

When the day had ended and the house was asleep, Zelda answered a scratching at her door. Without a word, they went to the window. Kidcou leapt and she climbed out, wary of her ankle. They brought the grasshopper's cage over to the cherry tree.

Zelda looked at the moon lying on the roof like a white whale. She'd been traveling for years in the space of one night.

"Show me how," Kidcou whispered.

Her finger over her mouth, she let her eyes wander around the circle to make him aware of the crickets in the neighboring gardens.

"I knew they were talking to the grasshopper. And the grasshoppper was talking to them. I somehow knew she made her music with a cello. It wasn't fair to keep her in prison." She carefully unlocked the cage door. "But I didn't open it right away. First I sang to her."

She cleared her throat. "Grasshopper, Grasshopper, talk to me. Trust me and I'll set you free. See? She's talking back. Gzzz-gzzz-gzzz. You try it."

"Grasshopper, Grasshopper, stay with me," Kidcou imitated Zelda's singsong, "don't go away when you are free." The grasshopper fell silent.

"Hm," Zelda said. "I wonder if we are sending conflicting

messages. You have to trust it, and go for it. All the way. Try again."

Kidcou tried. "Grasshopper, Grasshopper, if you come out, I'll follow you everywhere about."

"Bit of poetic license, huh?" She grinned. The grasshopper chirped. "She likes it. She's answering you."

"Couldn't it still be a he? I can't get used to — "

"Say 'he' as long as you like, moonsh — " She stopped herself. "It doesn't matter. And by the way, you don't have to croak like me. I know you can sing, remember? Now let's open the door."

Kidcou opened the gate with trembling fingers. Zelda rolled onto her stomach and laid her index finger down at the threshold.

"Do as I do. Good. Now let's sing together. Really sing. How about:

Grasshopper, Grasshopper, we want to see
you leap into the cherry tree.
Be with us now and be free,
take us both to Italy."

Kidcou sang it with her. "Hey!" He nudged her with his elbow. "Listen! Do you hear? You are singing on key!"

"Just go on singing, pesterbody!" She hated being interrupted. Anyway, she didn't believe him. As they sang again, and again, she heard Kidcou's voice. It was the voice that had been soaring through the church. The voice that had cut through the storm. Now it had a shine like the balls of crystal which he had taken out of his pocket and set down like sentinels at the corners of the cage. She heard him as though her ears were unplugged.

The grasshopper was probing the air with its antennae. It began to climb. Kidcou crinkled his nose. The insect was walking on his finger as if on a Sunday afternoon promenade.

Was she really singing on key? She was able to hear Kidcou and herself at the same time. He was adding little tricks and trills to the melody. She didn't falter. She sang on. Would her voice last? Would it hold out for even one more minute? Another night? Would she ever see the Grasshopper again?

"Take us both to Italy," she heard Kidcou's voice somersaulting beside her.

Make it happen, Grasshopper, she said in silence. Make it happen, Rower. She heard the words echo in her head when the vertigo struck. She grabbed Kidcou's hand. There was the wind. The rushing through her.

The grasshopper had leapt.

Zelda found herself in the cherry tree. And there was the Grasshopper in her dusty, old travel coat, holding the cello case. Her long, very long legs were leisurely crossed as though she had spent a lifetime in that tree.

Zelda saw that Kidcou was holding on to his branch for dear life. She reached over and gave his shoulder a squeeze.

"It's all right," she said, eyeing the Grasshopper to make sure it was. "Remember how you stayed up on that beam over the canal? Just hold on. Believe your eyes."

The Grasshopper was wearing Uncle Carlo's glasses. Zelda suddenly saw it clearly. It was the glasses that fooled you. Kidcou would only see Uncle Carlo in the Grasshopper's face. But she knew the glasses were hiding the Rower. The huge eyes were looking at both of them at the same time.

"*Grazzzie*," said the vibrating voice. "I admit, as the two of you must realizzze, I have been waiting for this." There was the cocked head and the fine, pointed smile. "Where did you say you wished to go?"

Kidcou was staring at Uncle Carlo's glasses, speechless. Zelda moved over and threw her arm around him to keep him steady.

"To Italy," she repeated for them both.

There was the chuckle of dry leaves. "Your faithful companion," the Grasshopper said with her familiar little bow. She waved her long, slender hand as though directing a course of thought, a course to take.

"To Italy. The winds are favorable."

THE END

EDGE
WORK

V EDGEWORK BOOKS began like this: a room full of writers — women, most in their fifties. Some had written best-sellers. Some were poets, most were therapists, or teachers of some kind. And all of them, once they started comparing notes, were worried about the shape and direction of the publishing industry. More and more, the really hot books were being turned down as "brilliant but too literary," "too feminist," "too unusual" to compete for market share. If this was happening to them, at the peak of successful careers, what was happening to the voices of emerging women writers? Who was encouraging, publishing, distributing, and marketing their best work?

EdgeWork Books began when this room full of women said, "We've got to have viable alternatives to the New York publishing machine," and one of them responded, "Well, if not us, then who?"

So that's us. We're trying to be the press we've been waiting for. We want to be part of the decentralization and democratization of the publishing industry — the structures that support it, the people who run it, and the work it produces. We publish well-written books with fresh artistic vision and, through our Web site, we offer supportive writing classes, individual writing consultation, coaching, editing, and open forums.

Please come join us — we look forward to meeting you online.

www.edgework.com

COLOPHON

This book was designed by Michael Brechner of Cypress House in Fort Bragg, California.

The text face and folios are in Lucida Sans, designed by Kris Holmes.

The title page, chapter and part headings are in Lithos, designed by Carol Twombly.